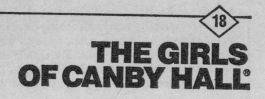

THE GIRLS
OF CANBY HALL®

18

MAKING
FRIENDS

EMILY CHASE

D0017822

SCHOLASTIC INC.
New York Toronto London Auckland Sydney

ISBN 0-590-40327-3

12 11 10 9 8 7 6 5 4 3 2 1   9   6 7 8 9/8 0 1/9

Printed in the U.S.A.   06

THE GIRLS
OF CANBY HALL®

MAKING
FRIENDS

THE GIRLS
OF CANBY HALL®

CHAPTER ONE

October Houston woke just as dawn was beginning to break over the Texas range. It was her last night at home on the ranch, and so she had spent it out here, as close as she could get to the sounds and smells and feel of the range, directly under its brilliant ceiling of stars.

Now she opened her eyes and saw the horizon edging from gray to blue, heard the last cries of two distant coyotes. She unzipped her sleeping bag and sat up, stretching her long freckled arms, running her hands through her curly red hair. Her horse Max snorted and scraped a front hoof on the hard ground — his way of saying good morning.

"Mornin', Max," Toby said, pulling a thermos out of her backpack. Last night's coffee was still warm inside. As she drank it, holding the cup in both hands, she watched the sun climb up over a distant mesa.

"Oh Max, how am I going to live without these sunrises? What can they possibly have out there in the East to compare? There's no room for the sun to rise out there. I looked on the map and Massachusetts is just a little bitty place. I'll die of claustrophobia. And living at a school with a bunch of wimpy Eastern girls. I'll bet all they do is polish their nails and eat little sandwiches with the crusts cut off. Ugh. Cranberry Hall in Green Rot, Massachusetts."

Toby knew that her new school was really called Canby Hall and that the town was Greenleaf, Massachusetts, but sarcasm was her only defense against having to go there. And she really dreaded going.

She had lived her whole life on ranches that her father managed. She loved the wide open spaces, and the solitude of living out here. She loved riding Max like the wind for miles and miles. She even liked helping her dad with chores. At fifteen, she already knew how to mend fences and birth calves and get a herd of cattle to high ground in a storm.

Her dad had taught her all this. They were close. Especially since her mother died three years ago. Since then the two of them had had to lean on each other for support. Through this they had developed a relationship of mutual respect. He really listened to her problems and ideas.

Still, when he put his foot down, that was it. And this summer he had decided that

Toby was going East to school. "To learn to get along with humans" was how he put it. He was afraid that, living such an isolated life out here, she was becoming a wild child. She didn't see this as a problem and so had begged him to let her stay. But he had stood his ground. And so for the rest of the summer she had put the move out of her mind, figuring she'd deal with it when the sad day came. Unfortunately, today was the sad day.

Tears started running down her cheeks. She wiped them away with her sleeve. She didn't like Max to see her cry. It upset him.

"Well, Maxie," she said in her bravest voice, climbing up onto his bare back, weaving her fingers through his mane to ride him back to the ranch house, where she could see the thin stream of smoke from the fireplace that meant her dad was up and had started breakfast, "we'd better get going. I've got a plane to catch this morning."

By the time Toby caught her flight in Dallas later that day, Andrea Cord was already on the last leg of her train trip from Chicago to Greenleaf, Massachusetts. She'd slept in a Pullman berth the night before, an exciting first for her, and she was seated at a window. Although her eyes were on the green and red and orange foliage of New England in early autumn, her thoughts were in the immediate future, trying to imagine what it would be like at her new school — Canby Hall.

Different — that was for sure. Her life in Chicago had been big city life — riding the elevated trains and meeting friends at the local places and working in her family's restaurant. Also, almost everyone in her neighborhood and school had been black, like her. At Canby Hall, she knew she would be one of a handful of black students. Would that make her an odd girl out?

Well, even if everything went totally wrong, she had only herself to blame. It had been her idea to go away to school. Her family would have much preferred she stay at home. But Andy knew she had to get out on her own, to find out who she was besides a Cord — a helper in the family restaurant, friend to her brothers, baby-sitter to her little sister. She loved her family, but sometimes she felt they were going to swallow her up completely. As her friend Judy had told her, "What you need is to go Cord-less for a while."

As the train left Boston, Andy started to get less nervous, more just plain excited. She pulled out her room/roommate assignment slip and looked at the names of the other two girls — Jane Barrett and October Houston — wondering what they'd be like, starting to imagine all the fun they'd have together.

Jane Barrett stood on the ladder, put the roller down into the pan, and pulled the paint-splattered kerchief off her long blond hair. She surveyed her work with satisfaction. It looked like she had succeeded in covering every last bit of black wall with classic Wedgwood blue — her favorite color.

For the past three years this room — 407 Baker House — belonged to Dana Morrison, Faith Thompson, and Shelley Hyde. At some point, these three had decided to be outrageous and paint the room totally black. This stunt had made the room famous — everyone on campus knew about 407 — but Jane couldn't imagine how they stood actually *living* in it.

Well, now the old 407 was a thing of the past, just like its inhabitants. Now Dana was living in Hawaii with her father. Faith was studying photography in Rochester, at the university. Shelley had gone back home to Iowa, where she was planning to major in drama at the state university.

Yes, Jane thought, now 407 Baker was a totally different place. For one thing, it was a single room this year — *her* room. She was going to be blissfully alone at last, a relief after a hideous freshman year trapped in a double with Gigi Norton (who Jane thought of as The Worst Person in the World). And so Jane had asked for a single this year, and was ecstatic when she was assigned — all by herself — to 407.

She'd spent the last two weeks of her summer vacation at home in Boston, planning how she was going to decorate the room. The Wedg-

wood blue walls were only Step One. Later
this afternoon she was going to unpack her
antique cross stitch quilt and her blue and
gray Persian rug. She had pale ivory curtains
for the windows. As soon as she got the
janitor to remove the extra beds and chests,
she was going to send for the pale rose velvet
sofa and white wicker coffee table she'd put
on order with her mother's decorator. It was
going to be a pastel retreat, an oasis of sub-
lime solitude.

"Hi there," someone said cheerfully from
behind Jane's back, roughly yanking her out
of her reverie. She turned to see a pretty black
girl standing in front of a huge pile of luggage.

"Yes?" Jane said in her coolest Boston
upper class tone.

"I'm Andrea Cord. But everyone calls me
Andy."

So? Jane thought. *Why tell me?*

"Nice paint job," the girl went on, nodding
approval, walking around the room over the
canvas tarps spread over the old wood floor.
"Hey. I'll help you clean up."

"Why would you want to do that?" Jane
asked, perplexed, looking down at Andy from
atop the ladder.

"Well," Andy said, "to be nice, for one
thing. And to get all this painting stuff out
of here for another. The sooner we get this
place cleaned up, the sooner I can get my
stuff in here and unpacked. I'm a neatness

maniac. I guess I should tell you that."

"But why should you tell me *anything*?" Jane said, stepping backward down the ladder. "And why would you want to move your things in here?"

Now it was Andy's turn to be bewildered.

"Why? Because this is my room! It's right here on my assignment slip." She turned and rummaged around in a duffel bag. Jane stared at the white lettering on the red jacket Andy was wearing. It said LEYTON HIGH CHEERLEADING. When Andy turned back around and straightened up, she handed Jane a crinkled green computer printout. Jane took it and looked it over. There, in black and white, under the heading "407/Baker" were three names:

Jane Barrett
Andrea Cord
October Houston

"Are you October or Jane?" Andy asked.

Jane gave her a frosty look and said, "My family wouldn't consider October an acceptable name. I'm not sure it even *is* a name. And I don't know what it's doing on this printout."

"I think she's our third roommate," Andy said helpfully.

"Third?!" Jane screeched. "There aren't supposed to be even two girls in this room. Only one. *Me*." She brusquely handed the slip back to Andy. "Well, there's simply been some dreadful mistake. If you'll excuse me for a moment, I'll go see the housemother and get this little difficulty straightened out. Then you can get those bags of yours into the right room and start to settle in. You must be tired, coming all the way from. . . ."

"Chicago," Andy said.

"Oh yes. The Midwest. Well, feel free to wait here while I get this all straightened out."

"Thanks a lot," Andy said, but her sarcasm was lost on Jane, who was already out the door.

CHAPTER TWO

When she got up to the top-floor apartment of Baker House, Jane's fury had built to the point where she felt like steam was coming out of her ears. The door to the housemother's apartment was open and the housemother — Alison Cavanaugh — was sitting on the big floor cushions in her living room, clearly in the middle of lending a homesick freshman a shoulder to cry on.

"And I m-m-miss by friend Alice, and my dog Camaro," the girl stammered between blowing her nose into Kleenexes from the box Alison kept on hand for emotional crises.

"Your dog's name is *Camaro*?" Alison said.

"Well, my brother has a Camaro and when the dog was a puppy, he'd crawl in and sleep in the backseat . . . oh he's so cute. I'd be feeding him his dinner right now — if I were *home*!"

Alison — an earthmotherly young woman

with wild, long brown hair and horn-rimmed glasses sliding down her nose, wearing jeans and a rose-colored rough cotton shirt — leaned over and draped an arm over the girl's shoulders.

"Believe me, Cindy, in a week you're going to feel better. But you'll have to put in a little work to get over the homesick blues."

"L-l-like what?" Cindy said, pulling out another handful of Kleenex to cover her sniffling.

"Did your folks give you any going-away money?"

"My dad gave me twenty dollars at the airport."

"Good. I want you to take that twenty and go get your new roommates and take them into Greenleaf tonight for dinner at Pizza Pete's."

"But what good will that do?"

"Believe me, I'm an expert in these matters, and I firmly believe that pizza is every bit as effective against homesickness as chicken soup is against the common cold. I'm thinking of writing a paper on this great discovery for one of the medical journals."

This seemed to calm Cindy down. Once she had left, still sniffling as she headed back down to her room, Alison told Jane to come in.

"What can I do for *you*? You don't look too homesick to me."

"Oh no," Jane said. "It's hard to be home-sick when you only live as far away as Boston. Besides, this is my second year here. I was in Addison House last year. I'm Jane Barrett." She held out a hand, which Alison shook.

Jane looked around Alison's apartment. Certainly different, she thought, taking in the exposed pipes in the ceiling painted red and blue and yellow. And the neon sign from an old beauty parlor that read KATIE'S KLIP'N KURL.

"Hmmm," Alison said, pushing her un-cooperative glasses back up her nose, "Barrett. Boston. Are you any relation to the Barrett who donated Barrett Hall here?"

Jane nodded and said, "Grandpapa. My family's been connected with Canby Hall for a long time. Which is why I know there's just been some silly mistake in the room schedul-ing. I asked for a single this year and was told I'd have 407 to myself. Imagine my surprise to find that two other girls — total strangers, transfers no doubt — have also been assigned to the room. Just a computer glitch, I'm sure. I don't want to bother you with such a minor error, but the first of these other girls just showed up with all her luggage. I'll need you to find someplace to put her."

"Let me have a look at the assignment sheets." Alison went over and rifled through the messy stacks of papers and books and magazines and balls of yarn and one sleeping cat on top of her desk, and finally pulled out a master computer listing. "Let's see. 407. Here it is. Jane Barrett. Andrea Cord. October Houston. Oh, there's a little asterisk here. 'See attached note. Patrice Allardyce.' Apparently our headmistress had something she wanted me to keep in mind about 407. I really ought to look at these things when they come through. Here's the note. 'Due to unanticipated heavy enrollment, there will be no single rooms at Canby Hall this term. All girls will have to share rooms until the overcrowding is diminished.'" Alison looked up at Jane. "Sorry. I should've come down and told you. Are you very disappointed? Were you really looking forward to living by yourself? It could get lonely, you know."

"I roomed with Gigi Norton last year," Jane said, by way of explanation.

"Is she the one who played that same Neil Diamond song for twelve hours straight?"

"Twenty-four. She wanted to get into the *Guinness Book of World Records*."

Alison nodded. "I get the picture. And I'm doubly sorry. And if there *were* a single room on campus, anyone who had lived an entire year with Gigi Norton would deserve it. But there simply isn't. You'll just have to get back into the idea of group living. And whoever these new roommates are, they'll have to be easier to get along with than Gigi. Look, you've already met the first one. How does she seem?"

"Chatty," Jane said bleakly.

"And look here. October Houston. With a name like that, she's bound to be an interesting person."

"Alison. . . ."

Alison grinned sheepishly and said, "I know, I should just shut up and let you be miserable."

"Oh, I've no intention of being miserable. I'll just have to go see Patrice Allardyce myself. If my grandfather gave an entire building to this school, I ought to be able to get one room in return."

"You know it doesn't work that way around here," Alison said firmly, walking Jane to the door. "Nobody has special clout at Canby Hall."

"We'll see about that," Jane said, turning away in a huff.

Patrice Allardyce wasn't in when Jane walked across campus to the headmistress' house. When she got back to 407, Andy was sitting amid all her luggage, reading an article about soap stars in the Chicago newspaper. Jane sighed audibly. It was impossible. How was she going to live an entire term with someone who liked soaps? (Though half the girls she knew loved them.) If she was going to be stuck with someone, why couldn't it be a girl who shared her interests — horses and ballet and writing and theater?

"Well?" Andy said, her voice still amazingly

full of cheerfulness. "Am I staying or leaving?"

"Uh, well, that's difficult to say," Jane said, a little rattled. "It looks like I won't be able to get this straightened out today. So for the moment, I suppose you can stay here. I wouldn't unpack everything, though. After I talk with the headmistress, I'm sure they'll be moving you to another room."

"Well, if that happens, I'll go along with it. But, to tell you the truth, I really like this room. I just love the view down onto the front lawn, with that cute little birdhouse and all the trees." Andy peeled off her jacket as she said this, then pushed up the sleeves of her black turtleneck and put her hands on her hips. "Don't mind me if I do unpack all this stuff. I just can't stand to leave things undone. These trunks will just haunt me if I don't take care of them."

And with that, she opened the first huge trunk and pulled out her bedspread and matching throw rug — both in an ultramodern print of diagonal earth-tone stripes. Jane took one look at these in the middle of her carefully planned classic blue room and burst out the door in tears.

Later that night, after Andy had had dinner in the cafeteria and Jane had gone into town for Chinese food at Ming's, they were both lying on their respective beds — silent, but dueling with tape cassettes. Jane had her mini-stereo on at the foot of her bed, playing Beethoven's Violin Concerto No. 1 — an old favorite.

Across the room, on her tape deck, Andy was playing a favorite of hers — Tina Turner's *Private Dancer* album. Neither of them could enjoy their music, of course. And the irony was that Jane loved Tina Turner. But she wasn't about to tell Andy that. And Andy loved Beethoven. She probably knew it even better than Jane did. She'd studied ballet in Chicago, and had danced to Beethoven in a recital last year. She wasn't about to tell Jane that, though.

Around ten o'clock, into this battlefield of silence and sound, came Toby, a long hard day away from Rattlesnake Creek, Texas. With mud still on her boots, she stalked into 407 Baker with a long duffel over her shoulder and an ancient beat-up leather suitcase in one hand. She didn't introduce herself or ask anyone's name, or comment on the oversupply of music and lack of conversation in the room. She didn't unpack or undress. She headed straight for the remaining bed, untied a green army blanket from the top of the duffel, unrolled it, took off her boots, pulled a Snickers bar out of her pocket, ate it, and then went straight to sleep in her jeans and fringed suede jacket on the bare mattress.

The other two just stared.

Oh wonderful, Jane thought sarcastically. A real live cowgirl.

Andy, flipping her tape deck off and snuggling down under her covers, had her own thought as she slid into sleep.

White girls sure are weird.

CHAPTER THREE

The volume level in the Canby Hall auditorium was roughly that of a Talking Heads concert. Three hundred girls filled every available seat, all waiting for the official start of another school year — the headmistress' convocation address. Just when the noise was at its peak, it fell away to almost nothing within seconds as Patrice Allardyce, cool and blond, smart but severe-looking in a beige, raw silk suit, strode across the creaking wood stage to the podium in the center. She rustled her notes and cleared her throat and took a drink of water from the glass on the stand, while the last voices from the audience fell away. When the silence was absolute, she began her address.

"Girls of Canby Hall. As the leaves rustle down from the trees here on campus, so do the pages of textbooks rustle open as another school year begins. . . ."

In one of the back rows, off to the side, sitting with a few of her friends from the choral group, Jane Barrett rolled her eyes.

Oh no, this is worse than last year's address, she thought, and tuned her mind to another station. She began working on what she would say to Ms. Allardyce after the address was over. An honest presentation of the facts, then a subtle reminder that Barretts rated preferred treatment around here. That ought to do the trick and get those two girls out of 407.

Meanwhile Andrea Cord — sitting on the other side of the auditorium — was so full of gloomy thoughts she could hardly listen to Patrice Allardyce's address. Just yesterday, she was so looking forward to meeting her two new roommates, hoping they'd be her best friends at Canby Hall. Today, neither of them was even speaking to her.

By now, Patrice Allardyce had run through the basic rules of Canby Hall, with emphasis on "ladylike deportment," which meant all sorts of things like not starting food fights in the cafeteria, or tap dancing on the row of washers in the laundry room, but most particularly it meant not getting overinvolved with boys — either the ones from Oakley Prep school down the road, or the "townies" — guys who lived in Greenleaf. To Patrice Allardyce, "overinvolved" meant anything more than arms-length dancing at school-approved mixers, or light hand-holding on campus. Kissing, for instance, was strictly forbidden in her book,

From this subject, the headmistress moved on to a more upbeat section of her address — celebrating the wonders of Canby Hall.

". . . and this year our administration and registrar's offices became computerized. I'm sure you all got your computer class schedules, which we hope will eliminate long lines and first-week confusion around here. You also have your computerized room and roommate assignments, by which we were able to match students in many sophisticated ways. Of course you don't really need me to tell you this. By now you're all enjoying settling in with roommates who share your interests and attitudes, beginning joyous friendships that will last through all your years at Canby Hall and beyond."

Andy and Jane, although sitting at opposite sides of the auditorium, groaned at this at precisely the same moment. Not October Houston, though. But that was only because, from where she sat — high atop a bluff overlooking Greenleaf — she couldn't hear a word Patrice Allardyce was saying.

What she was listening to were the sounds of the Massachusetts outdoors. This morning when she got up, she decided that as long as she was going to be stuck here for a while, she should at least try to make the acquaintance of the local inhabitants. And to Toby, the really interesting inhabitants of any place

were not its people, but its animals and trees
and flowers and insects.

To get to know them, she knew she'd have
to get very still and stay that way for as long
as it took to begin seeing and smelling and
hearing the secret life of the place. And so
she sat high up on this bluff in her jeans and
an old plaid shirt with the sleeves scrunched
up around her elbows, and felt the light fall
winds running light fingers through her hair.
She smelled the damp earth from the nearby
woods. She saw blue jays and cardinals on a
tree branch, a pair of rabbits hopping for the
cover of the woods, and a hard-working pro-
cession of ants making its slow, deliberate way
through the heavy wild grass where she sat.

She looked down into the valley that held
Greenleaf and Canby Hall. Much as she hated
being here, she had to admit that it *was* pretty.
Not wild and beautiful like Texas. Neater and
smaller and more tidied up. But pretty just
the same. What she heard as she looked was
an orchestra of a hundred creatures. But then
her ear began picking up something stronger.
She waited and closed her eyes. It was growing louder. Hoofbeats.

She turned and looked down the side of the
hill. There, coming straight at her from some
distance, was a horse so pure white and huge
she'd never seen the likes of it, not even at
county fair horse shows back home. At first
she thought it must be a wild horse, running
free, nostrils flared, saddle-less. But this was

a tame place, not the wild empty rangeland of Texas. This horse had to belong to somebody.

And sure enough, that somebody appeared on the horizon. It was a guy — tall and lean, older than she was, with longer hair than hers, blond. He was riding — and could he ever ride — a creamy palomino. But the runaway — bigger and carrying no weight — was faster. The guy couldn't catch up.

Without really thinking, more just operating on raw instinct, Toby stood up directly in the path of the stampeding horse, a filly. She stood absolutely still as it bore down on her, in spite of shouts from the blond guy.

"Get out of the way, you crazy kid!" he yelled. She didn't pay any attention to this. She knew exactly what she was doing. At the precise last split second, just as the filly was about to trample her, she jumped away, then up onto her back, grabbing her long white mane and pulling her head back to let her know who was boss now.

It didn't work. Nothing happened. The horse just kept galloping full-tilt, whinnying and snorting and throwing her head from side to side. At this point, Toby felt her nerve drain out the soles of her feet. Maybe this *was* a wild horse, some creature just shipped up from the Australian outback. Maybe she was the first human she'd ever had on her back.

I'm a dead woman, was the thought that raced through October's mind. Only fifteen, with so much to live for, and I'm a goner. Then she imagined the headline in the Canby Hall school paper. INCREDIBLY STUPID STUDENT KILLED IN IDIOT WILD HORSE STUNT. The possibility of being thought a fool by everyone at this twitty place made her crazy. She dug down deep inside herself and found some extra reserve of nerve she didn't know she had.

"I don't care if you're wild as the wind itself," she shouted at the horse, "if I say whoa, you're going to listen to me." And then for good measure, she pulled out her best secret horse trick. She grabbed the mane tighter and dug into the filly's flanks with her knees and leaned up and over until her mouth was pressed against the horse's head. And then October whispered something in her ear.

As if by magic, the horse slowed to a trot, then came to a complete halt just in front of a fence Toby had been afraid she was going to have to jump along with her.

For a moment she just sat there, breathing a little hard and thanking her lucky stars the trick had worked. Then she turned as the sound of approaching hoofbeats grew louder. The blond guy reined in his horse and pulled up beside her. At first he didn't say anything, just looked at her in wide-eyed amazement.

When he was able to put some words together he said, "I've never seen anybody do that before."

Toby blushed. The curse of being a red-headed person. Any time anybody said anything that flustered or embarrassed her the tiniest bit, she went pure pink. This drove her crazy. For one thing, it had forced her to give up playing poker with her dad and the ranch-hands. If she drew a royal flush, she got royally flushed and everyone at the table knew exactly what she was holding. Now, here, with this total stranger, she'd let him know he'd gotten to her. Which made it very difficult to play it cool.

She gave it a feeble try, anyway, saying, "Oh, it was nothing."

"Oh yeah, sure," he said. "You always just leap onto wild horses and whisper sweet nothings in their ears and turn them into little pussycats. I suppose on weekends — just for fun — you stop locomotives by tripping them with your foot. Hey. Just what *did* you say to that wild thing that got her to stop on a dime like that?"

"Oh," Toby said shyly, running her hand over the horse's long neck, soothing it, "I just told her she's real pretty. Horses are very vain."

First the boy looked at her in disbelief, then broke up, laughing so hard he had to wipe his eyes with the denim sleeve of his jacket.

"Where'd you ever learn that? Same place you learned to ride bareback, I suppose."

"Oh, I've been around horses for a while,"

Toby said modestly. "I come from Texas. I've lived on ranches all my life. Hey, is this horse really wild?"

The guy nodded and smiled and said, "One-hundred percent unbroken. We just got her in last week. You're a real Annie Oakley. I'm impressed." He held out a hand. "Name's Crowell. Randy Crowell."

She shook his hand and said, "October Houston."

"October?"

"I was born in the month of October. That's where the name comes from. Nearly everyone calls me Toby, though."

"Oh, I don't think I would. I think I'd call you October." He smiled this completely great smile. She felt it pour over her like sunshine. She wasn't used to feeling like this about a guy smiling. Of course her experience with guys was pretty limited. She had been smiled at by Duane Mills, who was the fattest boy in the county high school and was heavily into computers and smiled at everyone in an absent kind of way. She had also been smiled at once by Jeb Dean, who worked on the ranch with his dad and had two missing teeth. This smile had come just before he gave her a sudden kiss one morning when the two of them were out mending fences together. She had dealt with this by walking away and not speaking to him for a week.

This was a much different experience. She found herself hoping this guy would keep on smiling for a long time. Instead, though, he got suddenly serious and businesslike.

"Say," he said. "If you're used to working with horses, maybe you'd be interested in helping break this one in for us. For my family, that is. This is our ranch here. Probably a little smaller than what you're used to, but. . . ."

"Oh, I'd love to," Toby said, giving the filly another pet, then sliding off her back and walking around to get a better look at her. Then she caught herself. "The thing is, I'm supposed to be going to school, starting tomorrow. That's why my dad sent me here. I don't think he'd be too happy to find I'd come two thousand miles to do more ranch-handing. I think I'm supposed to be strictly Canby Halling."

"Oh," the guy said, growing suddenly colder in his manner. "Canby Hall."

"You don't like it?" Toby said. "Well, that makes two of us."

"Oh, I guess the school's all right," he said, getting off his horse to put a lead rope on the renegade one. "I used to know somebody there, though. It didn't end up too well. I've sort of shied away from the place since then. And now that I'm older, the girls seem like babies to me, anyway."

"How old are you?" Toby asked.

"Twenty!" Randy said huffily, and got back on his horse, ready to lead the other one back. "How old are you?"

"Fifteen," Toby said, trying to make it

sound older, but it didn't seem to carry much weight, even to her own ears.

"Well," he said. "I've got to be getting back. Thanks for catching this one, though."

"What's her name?" Toby asked.

"Doesn't have one yet," Randy said. "Want to give her one? Seems only fair."

"My own horse's name is Max. Could you call this one Maxine?"

He smiled his one hundred-watt smile again and said, "Sure. And hey. If you decide you've got any time left over from Canby Halling, the offer's still open. We're always looking for people who can really handle horses, even if they *are* just babies."

With that, he rode off, leaving Toby blushing again, but this time not with embarrassment. She was good and mad.

"*Baby*, eh?" she said out loud, even though he was already out of earshot. "We'll see about that."

CHAPTER FOUR

Jane leaned against the ivy-covered stone of the auditorium doorway, waiting for Patrice Allardyce to emerge so she could talk with her about her roommate problem.

Even if she wanted company in 407, Andrea and October — although not truly awful like Gigi (Worst Person in the World) Norton — were not who she'd choose.

For one thing, whereas Jane was naturally quiet and reserved, Andy was Ms. Chatterbox. She talked the way other people breathed. The only time she wasn't talking was when she was playing a tape from her large collection of rock and soul and disco. None of these were Jane's favorite kind of music.

Still, she knew Andy was just keeping the music going as a way of being lively and upbeat, just trying to be friendly with all her attempts at conversation. But Jane didn't *want* to be friends with her. She already had

all the friends she needed around here, mostly
girls from her private school in Boston, girls
whose families had known each other practically since the girls were born.

Still, even though Andy's persistent friend-
liness was annoying, Jane supposed it was
better than October's surly silence. This
morning, when Toby came back from breakfast — which she had eaten by herself at an
empty table way off at the far end of the
cafeteria — she walked into the room, stood
on a chair, and taped a teabag by its little
cardboard tab to the ceiling directly over her
bed. Jane had no idea what this was about,
and although she was a little curious, she
didn't ask. She knew she wouldn't get much
of an answer, anyway. Andrea had been trying to start up a conversation with Toby
since yesterday and so far all she'd gotten
were short, curt answers — usually "yep" or
"nope." Jane had never known anyone who
said yep and nope, never known anyone from
a ranch. She and October Houston couldn't
possibly have anything in common, and so
why bother trying? Especially since Toby
would be leaving 407 soon, anyway. Jane was
confident that Patrice Allardyce would take
care of that.

Unfortunately, when Patrice emerged from
the auditorium building, she wasn't alone.
She was engaged in an animated conversation
with Audrey Fortunata, the school's bursar.
Business talk. Clearly not a conversation Jane

could just break into. And so she began following them down one of the paths that crisscrossed the wooded campus. She tried staying a ways behind so she wouldn't look like a detective, but apparently she wasn't completely successful because — just as she entered the maple grove in the center of the campus — Patrice Allardyce turned suddenly and peered at her.

"Yes, Jane, hmmm?" she said. "Why is it that you seem to be following me? For a good reason, I assume. Or else I'm sure you wouldn't want to interrupt the important school business Ms. Fortunata and I are conducting."

It wasn't exactly the opening Jane had been looking for. Now whatever she had to say wouldn't seem good enough.

"Oh, that's okay," she said. "It was nothing really. That is, it can wait until you have a free moment."

"Yes. Well, you see it's the first week of the term. I'm not likely to have very many free moments for quite some time. So unless your business can wait until Christmas, I suggest you present it now. I'm sure Ms. Fortunata won't mind a brief interruption. I'm sure by now we're both curious as to why you've been following us all the way across campus."

This is going from bad to worse, Jane thought, but knew it would be her only chance and so plunged in with her story about the roommate mix-up. Patrice Allardyce said nothing all the while Jane was stating her case, didn't so much as flicker an eyelid to show what she was thinking. Then, when Jane was finished, Ms. Allardyce simply waved a hand to dismiss the whole matter.

"Jane, there's simply nothing I can do. We are filled to the rafters this term. A little problem with that new computer, or whoever programmed it. And so everyone's doubling and tripling up. Why I've even got one room in Charles House that has four girls in it!"

"Yes," Jane said, playing her trump card, "but then none of those girls are Barretts. I know I'm asking for special favors here. I don't deny that. But I do think that Barretts are special cases."

Patrice Allardyce looked Jane straight in the eye and didn't miss a beat before replying.

"You are so right, Jane. Barretts have always been special to Canby Hall. And always in the same way. For several generations now, your family has been very generous with its time and money. I'd go so far as to say that generosity is the true spirit of the Barretts. And so I know your parents would want me to remind you of this spirit by asking you to be even more generous than anyone else around here. And so if there's another late arrival today or tomorrow, I'll put her into your room."

And with that, she turned and motioned to Audrey that they should resume their walk, and the two of them were off, leaving Jane standing in the middle of the maple grove filled with rage and despair.

Then, to add insult to injury, down the path from the opposite direction came Gigi Norton. She was pretty, Jane had to admit that, with dark hair brushed behind her ears and big, brown eyes.

As soon as she saw Jane, her lips curled into a malicious smile. "Why, Jane Barrett as I live and breathe," she said in her Scarlett O'Hara voice.

"Hi, Gigi," Jane replied in her dead person voice.

"So sad you decided not to room with me this term," Gigi went on sarcastically. "It's so lonely in the old room without you. But I guess I'll just have to get used to living by myself. I suppose I'll manage somehow. Actually, I'm the envy of the entire dorm. Somehow the computer goofed and skipped right over my room, and I've got the only single in the place."

"You w-w-hat?" Jane sputtered, but Gigi was already doing a little spin and waving goodbye as she took off happily down the path.

Jane just stood very still and used all her inner strength to not run after Gigi and push her into a pile of dead leaves, or something else that very proper girls from Boston are not supposed to even think of.

While Jane had stayed after the convocation address to wait for Patrice Allardyce, Andy had walked slowly back to Baker, trying to appreciate the beautiful, warm, sunny fall day around her. She walked past the Main Building with the dining hall right next to it; past the library and science building. The rich smells and sights of Canby Hall's campus were so totally different from the urban landscape she was used to. Suddenly those old familiar sights and sounds and smells came tumbling in on her in a kind of random collage. The sight of el train tracks and stop lights and the brilliant colors of those snow-cone syrups in the dispenser jars on old Mr. Smith's cart. The sounds of radios from passing cars, her name shouted by friends from across the street. The smells of steaks sizzling in her family's restaurant, the beach along the lake in the summer.

She loved all of this, what she thought of as the life of her neighborhood. But she had also been looking forward to exchanging it for this completely different life, to being surrounded by maple trees and the smell of ferns and pine needles, and the sound of crickets through the night.

Now, though, try as she might, she couldn't enjoy a shred of it. She was just too upset at the situation in her room. How was she going to make it through an entire term with two girls, one of whom wasn't speaking to her and another who wasn't interested in speaking to *anybody*? She was so deep in these gloomy thoughts as she walked up to the fourth-floor hallway of Baker that at first, she didn't know what hit her. All she could tell, as she found herself suddenly flat on the hallway floor, was that her assailant was fast and blond and packed quite a wallop.

"Oh gee, I'm sorry," the assailant was saying to Andy. "Are you okay? Or did I kill you? I hope not. That would really get the term off to a bad start for me."

Andy smiled in spite of herself. It was nice to finally run into someone around here who shared her own offbeat sense of humor. And then she felt arms sliding under her own, lifting her to her feet, brushing her off, straightening her collar, tugging the bottom of her sweater back around her hips. She stood in a wobbly sort of way and turned half around to see a tall girl with a huge amount of long blond hair, with a wide grin on her face. Beyond her, at the end of the hall, was a bright red skateboard, now lying on its back, its wheels still spinning wildly.

"You look all right," the blond girl said. "Definitely not dead. I really am sorry. I guess I was kind of hanging ten, carried away on thoughts of California waves. And then suddenly there you were, right in front of me. Like the shark in *Jaws*."

Andy had to laugh. "And I wasn't even showing my teeth," she said.

"Oh great!" the blond girl said. "You can talk. A good sign. You probably don't have a concussion. I hope you don't have amnesia, either. Quick — what did you have for dinner last night?"

"Oh no," Andy moaned. "Last night was my first meal in the cafeteria here. I'm trying to forget it, not remember. Hey, aren't you one of the girls next door to me in 409? I think I saw you yesterday when I was coming in."

"Yeah," the girl said, offering a big smile and a strong handshake. "Diedre Adams. But you can call me Dee. I'm informal with all my victims."

"Andrea Cord. And if I don't have any broken bones, you can call me Andy."

"Hey," said Dee, "if you're not in a big hurry to get back to your room, why don't you stop by mine for a minute? Tell me what you think of my new decorating idea."

"Oh, I'm not in any hurry to get back to 407. If I got there by about next June that would be about right."

"My roommate hates it," Dee said, motioning Andy into 409 and pointing to the wall next to what had to be Dee's bed. It was completely covered with magazine photos of waves and surf and oceans and seas. The bed was pressed up against all this, covered in a cotton spread the color of sand.

"Well," Andy said. "It's original. I gather you like the beach."

"Like it?" someone said from the other bed in the corner. Andy turned to see a skinny girl with freckles and glasses. The girl went on. "She's insane on the subject. I think she's planning on wearing her bikini to bed, and putting on her suntan lotion before she goes to sleep. She thinks this will help her out of her homesickness. Meanwhile, though, I get to live in Massachusetts' most elaborate shrine to Laguna Beach, California."

"Don't listen to her," Dee said. "This is just her usual complaining. We've nearly got this problem sorted out. She's been much happier with me since I got rid of the fifty pounds of real sand I had spread all over the floor."

"Not a high point in our friendship," said the small brunette, who introduced herself as Maggie Morrison.

"But it looks like you two survived it," Andy said.

"Oh, Dee and I've survived worse than a bag of sand. This is — believe it or not — our second year rooming together."

Andy whistled low and said, "I'm impressed. I'm not sure we're going to make it through the first week in 407."

"You've got Jane Barrett in there with you?" Maggie said.

Andy nodded.

"My sister Dana sang in the chorale with her last year. She's one of the Boston Barretts. *Very* reserved and *very* proper. She's also probably a slob. Most of the really rich girls around here are. They're used to dropping everything wherever they please, and some-

body named Winston or Fifi running around
after them picking it all up. You just have to
whip those rich girls into shape on the slob
issue."

"I don't think I'm going to have a chance
to whip Jane Barrett into shape on anything.
The girl does not even *speak* to black girls
from Chicago."

"Oh, you don't think it's that, do you?"
Dee said, sliding her skateboard under her
bed and then flopping down on the sand-
colored spread.

"Don't know," Andy said. "Maybe. Though
she doesn't seem to like Toby any better, I
have to say."

"Who's Toby?" Dee asked.

"Our third roommate. She's from a ranch
somewhere out in Nowhere Junction, Texas.
So far she hasn't said more than two words
running. I guess out there they express themselves by roping steers and having gunfights
and smoking peacepipes."

"Oh, I know who you mean!" Dee said.
"I saw her coming in. Suede jacket with about
ten pounds of fringe. Stetson hat. I don't
think there were spurs on her boots, but I'm
not sure. She ought to shake things up a little
around here. I'll bet she's a pretty interesting
person."

"Well, she isn't being interesting to me,"
Andrea said. "Or to Jane, as far as I can tell.
Just stares and glares and says nothing. And
Jane just wants the two of us to politely disap-

pear. I gather she was expecting to have the room all to herself this year, and now she's pouting because she can't. Well, la-dee-da, I say."

"I can remember when my sister Dana started here as a sophomore," Maggie said. "She lived in 407, too. And did *she* have roommate problems. She and Shelley and Faith started out hating each other like poison. But they worked things out and were best of friends the rest of the three years they were here."

"But I doubt they were as different as the three of us are from each other," Andy said.

"Are you kidding?" Maggie said, shaking her head. "My sister's the big sophisticate from Manhattan. Shelley's from Pine Bluff, Iowa. Faith is a black city girl like you, only from Washington, D.C. No, they were about as different as three girls could be. Tell you what. I'm going to write to Dana. She's in Hawaii this year with our dad. I'll ask her how they got past their problems with each other. Maybe she can help, even long distance."

"Thanks," Andy said. "But I think I'm going to need help faster than your sister can get it here. The silence in that room is deafening. I think I'm beginning to hear echos."

"Well, we can help, can't we, Dee?" Maggie said, pulling her feet up onto the seat of her desk chair, wrapping her arms around her calves, and resting her chin on her knees as she thought. "I can try to talk with Jane. That ought to be good enough to start up a conversation. Maybe I can sound her out. It sounds like everybody in 407 is all bottled up. Too much feeling and too little talk to get it out in the air. I'll sic Dee on the cowgirl. She's good with difficult cases."

"Yeah, I'd like to meet her," Dee said. "And nobody can *not* talk to me."

"I don't know about that," Andy said. "We're talking about somebody who just hung a teabag over her bed."

"A teabag!?" Maggie said. "What's that about?"

"Search me," Andy said.

"Never fear," Dee said. "In fourth grade, I got Agatha Turner to talk to me, and she never talked to anyone, *and* she was really weird. She had seventeen ant farms in her room."

"And she became your closest little friend," Maggie said, guessing the end of the story.

"Are you kidding?" Dee said. "All she wanted to talk about was ants!"

The three of them laughed, and Andy started to feel a little better. Maybe she didn't have real roommates yet, but it looked like she'd made her first two friends at Canby Hall.

CHAPTER
FIVE

On weekday mornings, the dining hall, with its wide windows facing a green meadow, was technically open at six-thirty, but few girls managed to wake up and get down to breakfast much before seven. The students who worked in the cafeteria part of the hall generally used this slow half hour to eat their own breakfast and gossip a little. Except for the girls in the garbage disposal/ dishwasher room — informally known as The Wild Bunch — who killed the time with huge water fights using the dish spray hoses. Their squeals and screams could be heard all the way into the dining room.

Dee Adams had worked in the garbage disposal room most of her freshman year, helping to finance the huge long distance bill she always had from calls to a surfer named Steve back in Laguna Beach. This year she had been promoted out of the garbage disposal room, up to running the new doughnut machine at the end of the cafeteria line. She was supposed to drizzle circles of batter — or as close as she could get to circles — into the vat of bubbling hot oil, and then pull out the finished dough- nut a few minutes later with tongs, set it on a layer of paper towel and dust it with pow- dered sugar. She'd made samples for all the girls who worked breakfast, and now she was waiting for a few real customers to show up.

First through the swinging double doors into the cafeteria this morning — at six thirty-two — was October Houston, dressed in faded jeans, a maroon Western shirt with white piping, and a Stetson, looking like no one else at Canby Hall. Dee watched in amaze- ment as Toby took and put on her tray scrambled eggs, sausages, toast, fried potatoes, a short stack of pancakes, and two mugs of coffee. And then she was standing in front of Dee.

"You want to try a doughnut?" Dee asked.

Toby looked at her, then suspiciously at the doughnut machine, then back at Dee.

"Won't kill me, I suppose," she finally said.

"You're my first actual doughnut cus- tomer," Dee said, drizzling not quite a circle — more a squiggly oval — into the oil. The two of them watched as it puffed up and grew brown.

"I think you better pull it on out," Toby

said. "It still looks weird, but I don't think leaving it in's going to improve it much."

Dee laughed and retrieved it with the tongs.

"Looks like I need a little more practice," she said, grabbed what she thought was the powdered sugar shaker and liberally dusted the tangled lump of doughnut, then looked down to see it had turned completely black.

"Oh no!" she moaned, "I've got the pepper shaker!"

At this precise moment, Mrs. Sharp, Baker's stern head dietician, came by.

"Just checking how things are going with the new doughnut machine," she said, looking over Dee's shoulder, then growing ominously silent. "Would you mind telling me just what this pitiful specimen is supposed to be?" she said, when she was finally able to say anything at all.

While Dee was trying to come up with something good, Toby chimed in with, "Oh, I asked for it that way. That's how we eat our doughnuts back in Texas. I was so homesick for a good old Peppernut Special that I asked this doughnut girl here if she could just kind of whomp me up one. And mmmm, I must say it sure does look mighty good."

"It does, does it?" said Mrs. Sharp, who had been around teenage girls long enough to know most of their tricks. "Well, I'm glad. It always does my heart good to see a homesick

girl made a little happier. So please, go ahead
and eat it right here so I can enjoy watching
you enjoy your old down-home specialty."

Dee watched wide-eyed as Toby, without
a moment's hesitation, reached over the
counter, picked up the doughnut, and took a
large bite. Her eyes watered a bit as she hit
the pepper, but she managed to swallow and
smack her lips in an Academy-Award imper-
sonation of enjoyment and say, "Mmmm.
That's the ticket!"

And then she was gone, off to a table at the
farthest end of the room, leaving Dee alone
with Mrs. Sharp, who gave her a fishy eye and
said, "Well, all right, but no more special
orders, okay?"

"Okay, Mrs. Sharp."

Dee waited until the dietician had left, then
slipped out from behind the counter, went
over to where Toby was sitting, and sat down
across the table from her. "Hey. Thanks."

Toby looked up and said, "Aw, it wasn't
nothing. She looked like she was about to
make a little trouble for you. Thought I'd
just get in the way of that. No problem. I
should be getting some feeling back in my
mouth in a week or so."

Dee smiled. "You know, I think you live
next door to me. I've seen you around. I'm
Dee Adams."

"Toby Houston."

"I met one of your roommates yesterday."

Toby didn't say anything in response to

this, just dug into her eggs, which she'd covered with ketchup.

"Yeah," Dee forged on. "Andrea Cord. She seems real nice. I haven't met the other girl in your room — Jane Barrett."

More nothing.

"I gather you don't think much of your roommates?" Dee said, trying a new angle of approach.

Toby looked across the table at Dee blankly, and said, "They're fine with me. Neither of them snores loud or spits chewing tobacco. They say those are the real nasty ones to have in a bunkhouse."

"But what about being friends with them?"

"Is that required?" Toby said.

"Well no," Dee said, trying to hide her surprise, "but it does make life a lot easier. You know, fewer of those tense silences."

"Nothing tense about silence to me," Toby said. "I've spent my whole life alone, or with people who are used to being alone, too. Ranchfolk are pretty comfortable with silence."

"But wouldn't you like to make friends here at *all*?"

Toby took a long drink from her mug of coffee, wiped her mouth off with a paper napkin, and said, "Don't see much point in it, really. I probably won't be here very long."

"But you'll be here at least until June," Dee said.

"Maybe," Toby said cryptically.

Dee decided to give up. Trying to make conversation with Toby was like trying to surf on a waveless day. The girl clearly wasn't interested in friends, and so why force her? Dee was an easygoing Californian. She believed in letting people do their own thing. If being alone was October Houston's thing, so be it. She didn't look unhappy about it, and so why should Dee try to change her?

As soon as she got out of the cafeteria, as soon as she felt the double doors breeze shut behind her and was alone in the hallway, Toby gave a swift kick to the nearest object. Unfortunately the nearest object was a huge, unyielding coat rack, and so she wound up not only angry, but angry with a sore foot.

Why do I always have to be such a social moron? she asked herself. This perfectly nice person tries to make friends with me, and I act like I'm happy being a hermit, thank you. Well, I really fooled her. She'll never guess I'm just lonely and shy. None of them will ever guess. I'll live to be ninety and lonely and shy — but cool. I'm such a dope.

When Toby got back to her room, Jane was still asleep — sprawled beneath a tangled pile that was about half covers, half jeans and sweaters and underwear she hadn't put in the laundry or back in their drawers.

Andy was already up and dressed and on the phone. Long distance from the sound of

it. That was something new at Canby Hall
this year. There were phones in the rooms
for incoming calls. Calling out still had to be
done in a hall phone booth.

Andrea was saying, "Really. I'm *fine*. Hon-
estly. No, everything's great. Of course I miss
you all. No, I slept fine. Oh. That's too bad.
All of you? Up until three? Well, that must've
used up a lot of warm milk." She covered the
receiver with her hand and said in a low
voice to Toby, "My family. Kept each other
up all night crying because I'm gone. They're
being *awful*."

She took her hand away and went back to
talking in soothing tones. "Of course. Sure.
Put Baby Nancy on the line." She waited a
few seconds then said, "Ooooo Nancy Wancy.
Yes, Andy wuvs you. No Andy can't come
there. Andy far away. No no, don't start boo
hoo. No. Put Mommy on. That's a good girl."
She rolled her eyes at Toby. "Hey Mom, I've
got to go now. Classes start in five minutes
and I've got to run all the way across campus.
Yes, I'll call. No, not that soon. What about if
I wait until after lunch?"

When she finally hung up, she gave a sigh,
sheepishly, and said to October, "I seem to
have a unique problem. Practically everyone
else here is homesick, but with me it's that
my family is Andy-sick. It's a little embarrassing. Please don't make fun of me about
this."

Toby looked at Andy and, instead of saying something warm and friendly, was only able to come up with a terse "Okay," before grabbing her backpack full of books and heading out toward classes.

Andy shrugged as she watched Toby go out of the room. If her family knew how dismal things were in this room, they'd come with a helicopter and airlift her out of Canby Hall.

She turned back to see Jane still sleeping. There were only fifteen minutes left until first period classes began. What should she do? Jane hadn't asked for any help getting up. She should probably just let her be.

It'll serve her right for being so removed, Andy thought, sliding her fresh notebooks and uncracked texts into the high-tech clear plastic book bag she'd bought last week. She was almost out the door, when she turned around and went back into the room, and over to Jane's bed, and shook her by the shoulder.

"Mmrph?" Jane said, then burrowed deeper under the small mountain of clothes and bedclothes, and began breathing deeply and regularly again.

This time Andy gave Jane's shoulder a harder shake and accompanied it with a gruff shout. "Up and at 'em!"

This was a little more effective. Jane rolled over, opened one eye, and looked questioningly at Andy.

"You have — " Andy looked at her Swatch

watch " — exactly twelve minutes to get to class."

At this the other eye also snapped open. "What!? What happened to my alarm?"

"You looked disgustedly at it when it went off about an hour ago, slammed the snooze button about seven times, and went back to sleep."

"Oh, no," Jane said, leaping out of bed, rustling around among all the stuff on top of it, "how will I ever make it? How will I even find my socks in twelve minutes?"

"You might not find them in twelve years in the heap there. When you're in less of a rush, remind me to show you this modern invention — the drawer. It could really help." Andy *was* being sarcastic, but she meant it as a joke, a good-natured tease.

She was truly surprised when Jane turned on her with fire in her eyes and said, "Oh, why don't you just get out of here! Go to your classes, little Miss Neat-as-a-Pin-with-every-thing-in-its-place. I don't know why you even bothered to wake me up. You could have had a swell little joke, letting me miss my first class. Of course, then you wouldn't have had the chance to make fun of me."

"Jane, I. . . ."

But Jane had already grabbed her towel and was heading down to the lavatory to brush her teeth and wash up.

While Jane was rushing down the hall to-

ward the showers, Andy was running the
other way, off to her first class in tears.

Washing her face and combing the night
tangles out of her long curly blond hair, Jane
stood in front of one of the long row of mirrors in the fourth-floor lavatory and thought
about the encounter with Andy. Maybe it *had*
just been a joke. Jane was always a grump
when she first woke up, and she had doubtless put the worse possible interpretation on
Andy's remark. She probably owed her an
apology.

She rushed back to the room to say she was
sorry, but Andy was already gone.

Jane stood in the doorway and sighed.
Would this mess ever get straightened out?

CHAPTER SIX

Monday morning

Dear Judy,

If this letter looks like it's being written by a raving lunatic, that's because it is. I'm sitting here in my first morning study hall, steam coming out of my ears, trying to get myself calmed down, but your friend Andy is *mad*!

This girl in my room — Ms. Jane Barrett —doesn't think she just lives there, she thinks she owns the place! Her family came over on the Mayflower or something, and they're richer than the *Dynasty* clan, so she thinks we should all scatter rose petals in front of her when she walks around.

You'd think with all this hoity toity background Ms. Snooty would have all the best habits, but the girl is *El Slobbo Grande* (as we'd say in my Spanish class). Clothes? Hey, just drop 'em anywhere. I guess she thinks the

maid will come around and pick them up.
But there is no maid — only me tripping over
all her preppy stuff. (If Oxford cloth were a
toxic substance, we'd all be dead by now.)
And now she's furious with me for pointing
this little fact out.

The other girl in our room is just the opposite. She has almost *no* stuff and is hardly
ever around. Like a shadow. Her name is
October, which is cool. October Houston.
Skinny and redheaded with freckles and big
green eyes. She's from a ranch in Texas. She's
even related way back to Sam Houston. I
don't think she's used to being around so
many people at once. I'm not sure whether
she's shy or miserable, or both. Hard to tell.
She's not letting anybody inside that head of
hers. Comes in at night and crawls under
this ratty old army blanket like she's in a pup-
tent. She's got this teabag hung from the ceiling over her bed. I thought you might know
what that's about.

Anyway, you can see we're not talking
Ideal Situation here. Don't say anything to
my folks about this. If they knew, they'd send
a St. Bernard to rescue me. They call about
every ten minutes to make sure I'm still
breathing. I love them, but they are going
to drive me *crazy*! Somehow I've got to convince them that I love it here, and am really
okay, and am not coming home next week.

Except for the gruesome roommate situation, I really do like it here. It's so beautiful.

I want you to come soon so you can see all
the fall colors. Fall's a real season here, not
just the month between summer and winter,
like it is in Chicago.

What about boys? I can hear you asking.
Well, I don't know. Haven't seen many yet.
They're all in town, or at this boys' school
down the road. There's a dance there Friday.
Just might go over and take a look.

What else? Classes are hard, but not impossible. Teachers are looser than at Leyton.
Food in the cafeteria is positively inedible,
but they have a salad bar, and sandwich machines at the Student Center to ward off total
starvation. Dance space is good and the in-
structor — Sylvia Linden — used to be in the
American Ballet Theater company. She's hard
on us, but knows her stuff.

If only I could figure a way to get things
straightened out in the room. I can sense
that, if she just got off her high horse, Jane
might be okay. She's smart and knows a lot
about theater and music. She's real good with
makeup. You'd never even know she wears
any, unless you got about an inch away from
her face. All you know is that she looks real
glowy and great. I'd like to ask her for tips,
but she's never speaking to me for long
enough.

Woe is me.

Your faithful friend,
Andy

CHAPTER SEVEN

The first class after lunch on Jane's schedule was creative writing. This term, the course was being taught by Lily McArthur, a novelist who lived in nearby Avery. All the Canby Hall girls who were interested in writing had tried to sign up for the class and Jane felt lucky she'd gotten in.

Ironically, the class was on the second floor of Barrett Hall, a squarish brick building with a row of white columns in front. In the years since Jane's great-grandfather had donated the money for its construction, the dark green ivy planted around its foundation had crept over the entire structure. Inside, on this warm afternoon in early fall, the sun was streaming in through the narrow old windows, laying bars of light across the freshly polished wood floors. Stopping for a moment, Jane breathed in the wonderful mix of smells — floor wax and chalk dust and oranges and bananas and the colognes and cosmetics of a hundred hurrying girls. The frustrations of the past two days melted away as she felt an old familiar rush of excitement course through her. Another school year was beginning!

The writing class was small — only ten girls or so — and by the time Jane bolted in, they had arranged themselves in a loose semicircle. She was disgusted to see that Gigi Norton was among them. Gigi smiled her most sickening smile as Jane walked in, then held up her wrist and tapped the face of her watch. In a spontaneous moment, Jane crossed her eyes at Gigi and went over and took an empty seat on the opposite side of the circle.

Lily McArthur was talking in a low, clear voice. She was a striking person, with white hair drifting down around her shoulders, angular features, and pale blue eyes contrasted by a lined, deeply-tanned face. She was wearing black pants and a turtleneck, with two or three brightly colored scarves tied around her neck. Her fingers were heavy with a collection of turquoise and silver rings.

"There really isn't going to be any class this morning because this course will consist of *your* work. And so you need to go out and do some." She nodded to Jane as she came in, but didn't seem bothered that she was late, just went on speaking. "What I want you to do, as a sort of flexing exercise, is write something that takes you out of your ordinary realm of experience. Explore a path in the garden that you've never been down before."

"Uh, excuse me Ms. McArthur. . . ." It was Heide Hanson, raising her hand, although this was clearly the kind of class where you could just speak out. Heide was a junior and a notorious grind. She did everything by the book, and in those books highlighted more than she left unhighlighted. "Uh, just which garden on campus did you mean — the rose garden, or the Japanese tea garden?"

"Oh dear." Lily McArthur raised a hand to her throat. "You seem to have taken me literally. I only meant getting out of your usual settings and looking at something new. This will force you to bring something fresh to it. And then I want you to write on the experience."

"So it's a description of place you're looking for," said Carrie Halpern, a serious but nice senior.

"Yes," Lily McArthur said, "but more than that. I want your *impressions* of that place or event. I want it filtered through you."

Jane looked down at the lined page of her spiral notebook. She was holding her felt-tip pen in midair. She had written NEW PLACE? at the top of the page, but could not think of a single thing to write under the heading.

What kind of new place would be interesting? She realized that she never really went to new kinds of places, that what she liked best were old, familiar places. Her boyfriend Neal, back in Boston, was the same way. On dates they usually went for spaghetti at Sam's, a little Italian restaurant just outside the Back Bay area where both of their families lived. Then on to one of the art movie houses. On Sunday afternoons, they usually went to the galleries, or to one of the museums. When her family went out to dinner, it was usually to the Boat Club where the Barretts had belonged for generations. She just couldn't, for the life of her, think of a single place to write about. She half wanted to ask Lily McArthur for suggestions, but she didn't want to risk seeming as dull as Heide. Besides, by now, everyone was gathering up their books and milling out of the room.

"Good thing you weren't two minutes later. You would've missed the class entirely." It was Gigi, of course. Jane was determined not to let Gigi upset her.

"Why Gigi, you've changed your hair. The color, I mean," she said, changing the subject. Gigi was incredibly vain and always interested in talking about how she looked.

"Oh yes. Brown was so drab and boring. I had my mother take me to Elizabeth Arden over the summer and get Simon to do it black."

"Well, he certainly did a thorough job," Jane said. "It's definitely the blackest hair I've ever seen." She was hoping to plant a seed of uncertainty in Gigi's mind.

"Oh Jane, you are so behind. Don't you read *Vogue*? This is the absolute *latest* idea in color — vampire black. So, what are you going to write about?"

Jane felt caught off guard. "Uh, well, I think I'd really rather keep that secret for now."

"Well, I think you ought to go over to Oakley Prep Friday night. They're having a dance that's going to be totally new wave. They've got a great band — Ambulance — that's going to play. I'm sure you, Miss Jane Proper Barrett, have never seen the *likes* of Ambulance. I'd just love to hear your observations on that scene. It would definitely make for an amusing little paper. Well, sorry I can't stay longer and talk, but I'm off to geometry. Can someone please tell me why they're making me learn how to measure triangles? I mean, does this sound like something I'm really *ever* going to use in my *whole* life? I mean, *really*."

And she was off, leaving Jane still sitting at her desk. All the other girls had gone. Only Lily McArthur was left, sitting by herself on the deep white-painted window sill, looking down over the tree-filled center of campus.

Jane felt a huge blush creeping up her neck. She knew the teacher had heard every word of the stupid exchange between her and Gigi. The course had barely started and already Lily McArthur probably thought she was crazy for hanging out with someone like Gigi.

But when she turned toward Jane, all she said was, "Are you really so proper?"

Jane had to laugh. "I don't know. I guess so. Is that bad?"

"No. I just haven't met too many proper people. What's your name?"

"Jane Barrett."

"Oh, like this building."

Jane felt the blush deepening. "It's named after my grandfather."

"Oh. Did he do something heroic, or make a great scientific discovery?"

"He gave the money to build it."

"Oh," Lily McArthur said. "Are you very rich?"

Jane was taken aback. She'd never met anyone so direct. "Well, yes. I guess we are. But it doesn't get you everything you want, like people think."

"But it does make you a little proper," Lily McArthur said.

"Yes."

"What new experience are you going to write about? What wouldn't you tell your friend?"

"She's not exactly a friend," Jane said. "And I was lying to her. I don't know what I'll do."

"Why don't you take her suggestion then? Why not go to that dance on Friday? It sounds fairly interesting, and I definitely think you ought to try for something that isn't your usual cup of tea."

"*Me*!? I hate that kind of rock! And I'd fear for my eardrums. Plus, I'd die if anyone saw me there."

"Wear sunglasses then. Everyone does at those affairs, I gather. Really. I insist. I'm the teacher and I'm assigning you this dance as your scene to explore."

"You're trying to torment me," Jane said, but she was laughing.

"Of course not. I'm trying to push you outside of yourself a little."

"Okay," Jane said. "All right. I'll do it. I can't imagine that it will make a very interesting story, though."

That night, on the hall phone for outgoing calls, Jane told Neal about her prospective adventure.

"Oh Jane!" he said on the other end of the line in Boston. "I love thinking of you at this dance. I wish I could come there to take a picture. Send it to Ripley's Believe It or Not."

"Will you come and protect me?" she moaned. "I don't want to go alone."

"You know I would, Jane, but Saturday's the big race. Damsels in distress are one thing, but sailing is life."

Formally, Neal was Cornelius Worthington III. He and Jane had known each other practically since their nurses pushed them in baby carriages through the same park. Jane often thought how lucky she was to have found someone to love so early in life. She'd known she loved Neal in fourth grade. And how lucky she was to have the someone she loved so much like herself. It just simplified things. When you thought alike on nearly everything, there wasn't all that time wasted on disagreements.

"But I'll be with you in spirit," Neal was saying now. "I'll call you after the race. And hey — don't fall in love with any punkers."

They both had a good laugh at this. Jane had no idea then that, the next time they talked about the dance, neither of them would be laughing.

CHAPTER EIGHT

Canby Hall's campus, situated in a valley, had a particularly mild climate for its part of New England. Many September days were really more like summer than fall. Monday was one of these days. By the time classes let out, most of the girls were walking with their sweaters and jackets tied around their waists. Some of them were joining in impromptu softball games on the playing fields; others had changed into bikinis and were tanning on the lawns of the dorm buildings — Addison, Baker, and Charles Houses.

Jane's bad mood of the morning had turned around, through a happy day of seeing old friends from the year before, and finding that her classes looked mostly good. She got back to Baker and up to 407 feeling full of good will. A certain amount of this disappeared when she came into the room. She stood in the doorway, seeing where all her plans for a beautifully decorated solitary room had ended up.

No one room could be a bigger hodgepodge of styles. Against one wall was her own bed with its antique cross stitch quilt and Persian rug. Against another was Andy's earthtone geometric print spread and rug, topped with her enormous collection of teddy bears. On the wall over her desk were taped about a dozen magazine photos of famous ballet dancers.

Against the third of the three windowless walls stood Toby's bed. Since yesterday it had acquired a set of ancient, plain white (gone slightly to gray) Canby Hall sheets, patched in several places. Over them was the green army blanket. So far, Toby had no decorations or momentoes, nothing to personalize her space except, propped on her desk, a hinged dimestore picture frame. One side held a photo of a man who was probably her father, the other a picture of what was apparently her horse. She had a moth-eaten Navaho rug rolled out next to the bed, and the mysterious teabag was still hanging from the ceiling over it. That was it.

Seeing the clash of these three different styles — and the three different personalities they represented — lowered Jane's soaring spirits a few notches. How was it possible, she thought, that this would ever work out?

Into the middle of this thought walked Andy Cord. She brushed silently past Jane in the doorway, apparently still smarting from that morning's exchange. Jane followed her into the room and cleared her throat, trying to find a way to begin.

But just as Andy turned around, the phone rang. Jane was closest, and so picked up the receiver.

"Is Andrea Cord there?" a woman's voice said, between sobs.

"Y-y-yes," Jane stammered, panicked by the tragedy in the woman's voice. There must be some terrible emergency in Andy's family.

"It's for you," she said, hurriedly handing the receiver to Andy, patting her on the shoulder sympathetically, as she took it.

Jane knew it wasn't good manners to listen to someone else's private conversation, so she set about finding her swim suit in the drawers full of jumbled stuff she'd transferred Saturday from her suitcases full of jumbled stuff. Still, as hard as she tried not to listen, she overheard every word Andy said. It was nothing like the conversation she expected.

Andy's first response when she got on the line was to sigh with exasperation. "Oh Mom," she said, "it went fine. Yes, all my classes look good. No, the teachers aren't being mean to me. Yes, there's plenty of food at meals. No, I slept fine last night. No, I've really got everything I need. Of course I miss you all. Yes, I hear Baby Nancy crying in the background. I doubt that. I said I doubt she's crying because she's so lonely for me. She probably just needs her diaper changed. No, I don't have time to sing the Alphabet Song with her right now. It's time for extracurricular activities. Yes, they're very strict about that kind of thing here. I've got to be outside, playing at something in five minutes. Yes. Yes. No. Yes. I love you, too. Bye."

She hung up and exhaled hard. "Next time could you just say I'm out of the room?" she said to Jane.

Jane shook her head in disbelief. "You must be the greatest kid in the world for them to miss you this much."

"Oh I don't know about that," Andy said modestly. "I think maybe they're just the craziest family in the world."

"You know," Jane said hesitantly, "I came back to the room to apologize to you this morning, but you'd already gone. I didn't mean what I said. I have the disposition of a cobra when I wake up. Especially when I find out I'm running late."

"Oh, that's okay," Andy said, then thought, *Why do I always say 'That's okay' whenever someone apologizes to me? Even when it isn't okay at all?*

Just then Rita Martin, who lived about four rooms down, came into the room bent over double, pushing a huge, apparently heavy, cardboard carton.

"This came to our room by mistake," she

said, panting as she stood up, rubbing the small of her back. "Think it belongs here," she said, then left.

Andy went over and read the label. "Uh oh."

"What?" Jane asked.

"I'd forgotten about this," Andy said. "When I was leaving, my folks told me they'd put together an emergency kit and had sent it out here ahead of time. It's supposed to be filled with everything I'll need and might not have out here."

"Oh! Open it!" Jane said.

"This might be embarrassing."

"I promise I won't laugh."

They found scissors and cut through all the layers of tape wrapped around the box, then pried the top flaps open.

Andy pulled out the first of the newspaper-wrapped objects packed within.

"Thermal underwear," Andy said, unrolling a long set with attached feet. "Just in case winter rolls in about three months early, I guess. Go ahead, you get to open the next one." She nodded at Jane, who pulled out a long, tube-shaped object.

"Eight rolls of toilet paper," she said in amazement as she unwrapped it.

"They think Greenleaf is a remote wilderness."

"I think I'm beginning to get the picture," Jane said.

"A dozen bottles of homemade barbecue sauce," Andy said, opening a smaller box inside the larger carton.

"What's that for?" Jane asked, bewildered.

"Oh, my family lives and dies barbecue. They own one of the best steak and ribs restaurants in Chicago. Our sauce is a deep family secret. Maybe there's a miniroaster down in here somewhere so we can make our own ribs here in the room."

"Oh, that'd be great," Jane said, sarcastically. She felt her anger returning at the thought of barbecuing going on in the room. Next thing, the cowgirl would be brewing coffee over a campfire in the middle of the floor.

"You don't like ribs?" Andy was truly mystified.

"I don't believe I've ever had them. Unless you mean *prime* rib."

Andy had to laugh. "No, girl. I do not mean prime rib. I mean *ribs*. But I guess I can't expect you to know about something like that."

Jane looked wounded, and didn't say anything. Andy immediately felt bad. She saw that after thinking Jane so snobbish, now she herself was doing the same sort of thing — being smugly black in opposition to Jane being smugly upper class. But she couldn't, at the moment, think of a way out of this tangle, and so just tried to change the subject.

"Hey, have you figured out what the teabag is all about?" She pointed to it hanging from the ceiling.

Jane shook her head. "I don't know. Maybe it's some weird thing they do out there in Nowhereville where she comes from. You know — to ward off the evil coyote."

"Or keep away the killer tumbleweed," Andy suggested.

Neither of them heard Toby coming in the room behind them, until she brushed past both of them, dove into her bed, and pulled the covers up over her head.

The other two looked at each other sheepishly. For sure Toby had overheard them.

"Hey," Andy tried first, talking to the lump under the blanket, "we're sorry. We were just curious about your teabag, and started guessing what it means, and well, I guess we got a little carried away."

The lump didn't move.

Jane chimed in, "We didn't mean anything, well, anything negative by it.

The lump continued to play dead.

Jane and Andy looked at each other. They didn't know what more to do. If Toby was sulking, they apparently weren't going to be able to cajole her out of it. If she was trying to take a nap, they didn't want to disturb her.

"I guess I'll go outside for a while and catch a few rays," Jane whispered to Andy when she finally found her swim suit deep in her sock drawer.

Andy waited for Jane to ask, "Want to come?" but Jane didn't.

Andy's face tightened with hurt.

"Now what have I done?" Jane asked. Andy said, trying to keep her voice from shaking, "I thought you might have invited me along."

Jane was startled. "I'm sorry, I didn't think you'd . . . I mean, sunbathing. . . ."

Andrea said stiffly, "Black people *do* lie in the sun, you know."

Neither of them said anything more. Andy went down to the machines in the basement to get a Coke, thinking what an insensitive creep Jane was. Jane put on her suit in silence and left the room carrying her beach blanket, thinking, Give me a break. So I didn't know. If she's going to be that oversensitive, there's no possibility we can be friends.

As Andy pushed her change into the machine and waited for the Coke to come thudding through, and as Jane walked out onto the front lawn of Baker squinting at the bright afternoon sun, and as Toby curled up in the darkness under her blanket, all three had the same thought about the situation between them.

Back to Square One.

CHAPTER NINE

The next morning, Toby was the first girl awake on the entire Canby Hall campus. From her years on the ranch, she had developed the habit of waking with the dawn. She was lying very still in her bed, eyes wide open, all her senses focused on the day just beginning outside the lace curtains Jane had hung at the windows of 407. She felt the day calling to her, and so she slipped silently out of bed, touching her feet to the morning-cool floorboards. She stealthily got into a pair of jeans and an old favorite rough-woven cotton sweater. She pulled on her boots, slung her backpack over her shoulder, and was out the door. Carefully, she filled in the blanks on the signout sheet taped on the outside of the door. She wrote her name, where she was going, and what time she'd be back, leaving blank the space she had to fill when she returned.

Outside, the campus was utterly still except for the dry rustling of red and orange leaves, and the short songs of birds in the branches. Toby created a streak of raw energy through this tranquil landscape as she ran past Addison House dorm and the wishing pool, past Patrice Allardyce's house, along the path around the old pond, and off in the direction of Crowell horse farm.

Not that she really *knew* that this was where she was going. Well, maybe her feet knew first, but the information hadn't reached her head yet. Not until she had crossed over the ridge and walked by the bluff where she'd met him, did she start to realize what she was doing. She had simply written Greenleaf on the signout sheet. She *hated* the sheet, hated the feeling of confinement it gave her.

When she came over the second ridge — moving fast with her long-strided walk — there it was, the Crowell farm. She wasn't sure how she knew this was it, but she was. The farmhouse was painted a deep blue-gray trimmed in white — New England colors. You'd never find a ranch house in Texas painted like that. Behind it, the barn was bright red against the green, rolling pastureland and the blue sky with soft white clouds. She had to admit it was awfully pretty.

The main corral was in front of the barn and held about twenty-five horses. Toby spotted Maxine right away. There weren't many horses so absolutely white, and even fewer so wild and arrogant-looking. While the others wandered aimlessly around the corral, or stood docile at the fence, Maxine snorted and hoofed the ground, and tossed her mane, and broke as close to a gallop as she could in such a confined space.

Toby walked down the slope, toward the corral. When she was nearly there, the screen door at the side of the house swung open and there he was, looking even better than the picture she had held in her memory these past days — his blond hair tumbled around the collar of his faded chambray workshirt, his features so chiseled, his expression so intense, she was reminded of James Dean.

He didn't seem at all surprised to see her. He walked at a pace to match hers so that they met at the fence of the corral.

"Come to visit your friend?" he said.

She nodded. It *was* partly true, after all, that she had come to see the horse. And it was the only reason for being here that she could admit to.

"Looks like she needs to stretch her legs a little," she said.

"Yeah," Randy said, pulling out a tall piece of grass and chewing on it thoughtfully, "I was thinking the same thing myself yesterday. But there wasn't anyone around who had the nerve to get up on her back. My brothers all call her 'Suicide Mission.' I told them I'd met a girl who rode her like she was a merry-go-round pony and they thought I was making it up. So, if you want to give her another try, be my guest. I'd love to see my brothers' jaws drop when you swing into the saddle."

"Oh," Toby said, "I won't be needing a saddle. After these few days cramped up in that girls' school down in the valley, what I'm needing is a wild ride on a wild horse."

Randy shook his head. "It was one thing you riding her bareback the other day. You were acting impulsively in an emergency situation. But this is different. I can't take the risk of letting a young girl out on a wild beast like that, without so much as a bridle and saddle."

Toby planted her feet apart in a defiant stance, put her hands on her hips, and glared at Randy with fire behind her green eyes.

"*Young girl,*" she said, spitting the words back at him. "I'll have you know I've been riding horses since I was four. I've ridden every kind of horse there is — mares and fillies, geldings and stallions, Arabians and quarterhorses. I've even been on a few Shetland ponies. I've ridden English and Western and once for a laugh I rode sidesaddle. I've broken horses and trained them and jumped them in shows. If there's anything about horses I don't know, it isn't worth knowing. You may have your own farm here, and you might have a few years on me, but I'm telling you that you can just wipe that look of concern off your face and let me take that big bad horse of yours for a ride."

For a moment that stretched out with the tension in the air, the two of them stood silently looking at each other.

When Randy finally broke it, it was to say, "All right." He sighed in resigned defeat, then slid into a slow grin. "And I'm sorry about the 'young girl' remark. But I still want you to try a bridle on her. It's time we started getting her fit for riding."

Toby gave in, nodding. Although she'd been full of nerve in defending herself, she found herself suddenly floundering with shyness in the face of his smile. This was ridiculous. What was going on here? Since when did she have trouble talking horses with ranchers? Whatever was going on inside her was completely new, and while it was partly a kind of good feeling, it was also all jumbled up and confusing. She liked things simple and clear, and her thoughts about Randy Crowell were anything but simple or clear. Since she couldn't make any sense of them, she tried her best to push them aside for the time being.

"Well, if you'll excuse me then," she said, walking past him toward the corral, "I'll just get me a horse here. I've only got an hour or so before my first class, so I won't run off with her. And I'll cool her down good before I bring her back."

"You know," Randy said, stretching his muscled arms above his head and yawning a little, "I could use a short ride to shake myself awake this morning. Would you mind a little company?''

Toby's shyness receded for a moment as she smiled at him and teased, "Not if you can keep up the pace."

They raced each other for the corral, laughing all the way, and leaped over the fence. Toby found Maxine, and stroked her neck, and whispered a few words of flattery in her horse ear, and slid onto her back, as if she'd been riding her for years. Maxine didn't seem to mind at all. Randy stood in amazement watching this, then ran through the corral into the barn to get his own horse. With no time to saddle up, he was forced to ride bareback, too. Still, by the time he came out of the barn on the back of his palomino, Toby was already a distant figure, just about to ride over the crest of the ridge.

But then she stopped and turned her horse and held her still, waiting for Randy to catch up. When he got within shouting distance, she yelled out to him, "Come on, slowpoke! We haven't got all morning, you know." Then she laughed again. And got him to laugh at himself, as the two of them began to ride hard across the foothills, their horses matching each other's pace. Both they and the horses were breathing hard by the time they reached the small forest that bordered one side of the Crowell ranch.

"We'll have to slow them down through

here," Randy said. "Too many low branches."

So they walked the horses through, riding side by side most of the way, not talking much, which was fine with Toby, just enjoying the morning together. And the morning was really happening by the time they got into the forest. The sun was coming in through the branches in hard streaks, alternating with cool dark patches. The woodland scents, from the maples and the crabapple trees especially, made Toby feel better than she had in days.

"You know," she said to Randy, "your outdoors here is nothing like mine back in Texas, but I'm still at home in it."

"I think I know what you mean," he said, wiping the sweat from his forehead with the sleeve of his shirt. "I think there are indoor people and outdoor people, and the outdoor people are more comfortable in any outdoors than in any indoors." He stopped and laughed at himself. "Am I making any sense?"

Toby nodded laughing. "I know what you mean. I'd rather be outside anywhere. If I go too long without some ground under my feet and some sky over my head, I get feeling like a prisoner. I've got five classes a day at Canby Hall. Sitting at a desk all that time drives me crazy. The only time I get to stretch out is in this stupid aerobics class I'm in. And all we do there is hop around the gym like a bunch of jack rabbits."

"Why'd you take it, then?" he asked.

Toby felt herself blushing again. "Well, that's a little embarrassing. Fact is, I thought aerobics meant flying lessons. I thought they were going to teach us how to pilot planes."

He laughed and mused, "I can just imagine flying lessons at Canby Hall, with all the beginners grazing the top off Patrice Allardyce's house."

"You know Ms. Allardyce?"

"Well, sort of. I think I told you I used to hang out at Canby Hall a lot. I was dating a girl who went there. Dana Morrison. She lived in Baker house."

"Me, too," Toby said. "What room was she in?"

"407."

Toby whistled. "What a coincidence. That's where they've stuck me."

Randy slid off his horse. They were into fairly dense woods by now. Toby did the same. They started walking together, between the horses.

"Is the room still painted black?" he asked.

"Black!? No, it's this sickening blue. One of my roommates did it." She stuck out her tongue to show her opinion of the color. "So, this girl friend of yours, Dana — she's gone now?"

"Mmmhmm," he said, "she graduated and went to Hawaii. And she's not my girl friend anymore. That's been over for a while now. I haven't been on your campus since. I decided not to tangle with any more Canby Hall girls. Let them date those Oakley Preppies. They deserve each other."

"Sounds like you're still kind of mad at this Dana," Toby said.

"Oh, forget I mentioned the whole thing," he said brusquely, shutting down on the subject. "What can you know about love, anyway? You're just a kid."

"You say that once more and I'll have my horse bite your horse."

Randy laughed.

She couldn't tell if he was serious or teasing about her age, if he really thought she was just a kid, or was just trying to show off how much older and wiser he was. She didn't feel like there was that much difference between them. In fact, he thought more like her than anyone she'd met in a long time. That had to mean more than some stupid age difference.

When they got back to the farm, she pulled her watch out of the backpack she'd left dangling over a fence post.

"I'm five minutes late already. Even walking fast, I'm going to be twenty minutes late by the time I get to Spanish class."

He thought for a moment, then remounted his horse and, reaching down to give her a hand up, said, "Come on. Hop on behind me. I'll give you a ride."

They covered the distance at a full gallop. To keep her balance, Toby had to put her arms around Randy. Holding onto him like this, the beat of her heart quickened. Another surprise. She couldn't remember this ever happening before.

He rode her all the way to Stuart Hall, where her Spanish class met. She could see through the end window on the ground floor that Mrs. Harry was already pacing up and down the room, putting the girls through a drill. On adjectives, probably. Toby had meant to study them this morning. It was only the first week of term and she was already behind.

She slid down off Randy's horse, patted its neck, and tugged at the cuff of Randy's jean leg as a silent way of saying good-bye.

"Hey," he shouted when she was almost to the door of the building, "any time you need a hunk of outdoors, I can probably spare you some."

"Thanks," she said and smiled.

There was no sneaking into class. The door was at the front of the room. And so she apologized to Mrs. Harry and slunk up to her desk, which was in front of Dee Adams'.

Before she'd even found her place in the book, she felt Dee tapping her on the shoulder.

"Nice entrance," she whispered. "Being delivered to the door by Sir Galahad. Now reach behind you. I've got a present."

Toby did as she was told and felt a heavy,

solid packet wrapped in foil thrust into her hand. She brought it up slowly onto her lap and undid the aluminum. Inside were two doughnuts, still warm.

"I skipped the pepper this time," Dee whispered. "Hope you're not disappointed."

Toby felt two tears coming up, one in each eye. She rubbed them away fast. Back home, she prided herself on being independent and tough, but here she was going all soupy as soon as someone was nice to her, acting like she wanted to be her friend. And what was her big shyness problem with Randy? What was happening to her?

Must have something to do with the change in time zones, she thought.

CHAPTER TEN

As the first week of the fall term passed, the three roommates developed routines of coming and going that gave them as little contact with each other as possible.

Toby was up and gone before the other two awoke in the morning. Andy and Jane's alarms went off around the same time, but Andy got out of bed and was ready right away while Jane burrowed in with her pillow over her head, punching and repunching the snooze alarm button until the last possible minute. By the time she actually got up, Andy was usually on her way to classes.

The only overlap they had in schedules was an American history class that Toby and Jane shared. But the teacher — Mr. Benson — assigned seats alphabetically, and Barrett and Houston were halfway across the room from one another.

Jane ate lunch with friends from the

previous year. Toby took to sitting with Dee and Maggie. Andy generally skipped the meal. She found that the dance studio was empty between noon and one, and so she brought along a carton of yogurt and a granola bar, and worked at the barre for the hour. She was determined to eventually dance in a major ballet company, and knew that was going to mean years of giving up things like hanging out in the Baker cafeteria, making friends, gossiping over cups of coffee and milk, like nearly everyone else.

After school, Jane studied in the library. Andy came back to the Baker lounge, loving its overstuffed sofas and oriental rug. Toby took her books under some out-of-the-way tree, and tried to keep up with the piles of homework the Canby Hall teachers handed out. They assigned way more than she was used to at the Harmon County Consolidated School back home, where the teachers accommodated for the fact that most of the kids had to work afternoons on their family ranches.

At night, Toby went to sleep early, pulling the covers over her head to shut out the rest of the world. Sometimes, Jane would play a classical tape turned down low. Sometimes Andy would play a little rock, but they didn't war with their music anymore. Rather, they observed elaborate rituals of politeness. It was as if nobody wanted to be first to trigger off the next battle. This got to the point where the three of them mostly tried to not be in 407 at the same time, except for when they were sleeping, or getting ready for bed. When they were just hanging out, the silence got too loud.

One night, Alison Cavanaugh stopped by, making her first-week rounds to see that the girls in Baker House were settling in all right.

Toby was already asleep. Andy was studying herself in the mirror, mentally debating whether she ought to spend some of her summer savings to get a wonderful haircut. Jane was sitting at her desk, puzzling out a paragraph in *Le Petit Prince*, the book they were reading in her second-year French class.

When Alison appeared in the doorway, Andy and Jane both looked up, startled. Room 407 didn't get many visitors.

"Wow!" Alison exclaimed, completely misreading what she saw. "What a quiet, well-behaved group. It's nice to see a room where everyone's already so clearly comfortable with each other. I'll just move along, then. No sense asking if everything's okay here." Then she stopped. "It almost seems *too* okay here."

Everyone except Alison knew what was going on in 407. While the other girls on the floor were decorating their rooms together and making friends, and going into Greenleaf to the movies or for pizza, 407 was a tomb of silence. It was becoming known as "Baker's Bermuda Triangle." The other girls on the floor — except for Maggie and Dee — steered clear of its gloomy atmosphere.

In spite of this gloom, Andy was whirling with excitement Friday night. Like most of the girls at Canby Hall, she was getting ready to go to the Welcome Back Dance at Oakley Prep.

Andy was a dancer. Whether it was ballet or rock, she was equally good at both. Dance floors, with their plays of light and music, were her place to stand out. She knew how good she looked in motion. She didn't know what these Oakley Prep guys would be like, but if any of them liked to dance, she'd have a good time tonight.

Andy came back to 407 fresh from showering and, while her hair was taking the heat from her hot rollers, she sprayed herself with a healthy shot of L'Air du Temps, humming along to the Grace Jones tape she had on her deck, which was sitting on the dresser. She danced lightly around the room as she got into her soft dark brown pants and a beige V-neck. She put dangly earrings in the one hole in her right ear and the two in her left.

She was nearly ready before she noticed that she was the only one in the room who *was* getting ready. Toby was sitting up in bed, in her jeans and an old gray sweat shirt, reading a book on quarterhorses. Jane was at her desk. It looked like she was studying her biology text, but she seemed restless and distracted. She kept looking up and out the door as girls would go by on their way out, laughing and talking in pairs and small groups.

"Must be hard trying to study around here on Friday nights," Andy said to Jane, just to cut the silence a little.

"Yeah," Jane admitted," everyone gets pretty rowdy."

"Why don't you give up then — both of you — and come along with me to the dance?"

"No thanks," Toby said and went back to her book.

"I already have a boyfriend, thank you," was Jane's response.

"So what?" Andy said. "I mean, boyfriend hunting is only one of the things dances are great for. I myself — although totally boyfriendless at the moment — am not going over there with that on my mind at all. Well hardly at all. But I am mainly going to *dance*!"

"Well, I don't dance much," Jane said, "but I was actually thinking of going over for the cultural experience. Our creative writing assignment is to write on some place or event we've never experienced before."

"And you've never been to a dance?!" Andy was clearly incredulous.

"Well, a few evenings at the Boat Club," Jane said. "Cotillions and such. But not a hard-rock-night-in-the-gym sort of thing. No, I can't say that I have. It's just not my style, I'm afraid."

"Then you just *have* to come," Andy said, her natural enthusiasm overriding her usual hesitancy around Jane. "You can be the anthropologist. You know, like Margaret Mead going to Samoa. This dance can be your foreign territory. Would you take notes?"

She was only kidding and so was stunned when Jane pulled a small spiral notebook out of her desk drawer and said, "Of course."

Oh boy, Andy thought. This girl is something else.

"If you can wait a few minutes," Jane said, shyly, "maybe we could walk over together."

"Uh, okay," Andy said. She wasn't particularly crazy about being at the dance with someone standing there taking notes. On the other hand, it was the closest to an invitation she'd yet to get from Jane. If she was making a gesture of friendship, Andy didn't want to squelch it.

And so, twenty minutes later, the two of them were on the winding paths of the Canby Hall campus, among all the other girls on their way to Oakley Prep, which was just down the road. The dance was being held in the gym at the boys' school. As Andy went in, her first thought was a reassuring one. Things weren't all that different out here in the East.

"I think I'll know I'm a grown-up," Andy said to Jane, "when I get to go dancing someplace that doesn't have basketball lines on the floor."

Jane smiled politely, but Andy could tell she really didn't quite get it.

The dance was the first social event of the fall term and so was full of students from both schools. Those who had been there awhile referred to this as "Checkout Night" because everyone came to check out who was new this term, and who'd come back and how they'd changed.

There was a group up on a portable stage — Ambulance, Oakley Prep's Hottest Band, as it had been advertised all week on flyers tacked to practically every tree on campus. Andy could tell within moments of coming into the gym that they were really good.

"Loud, aren't they?" Jane shouted at Andy.

"That's the point," Andy said, nodding.

Jane pulled out her notepad and began scribbling furiously. Andy thought she was going to die of embarrassment. Usually only her older brother, Charles, could make her feel like she was going to die of embarrassment, and he was usually *trying* to make her die of embarrassment. Like when he xeroxed a page out of her diary and gave it to Cornell Smith, the boy whose "dreamy brown eyes and sweet smile" Andy had been writing about. But Jane was making Andy want to dig a hole and climb in, without even knowing she was having this effect. It seemed that everything she saw going on at the dance was important to write down. She had stood there through two numbers scribbling nonstop, oblivious to the growing number of kids who were giving her strange looks.

"Hey," Andy said, tapping Jane on the shoulder, then shouting in her ear. "I'm going to dance now."

"Where? I mean with who? I mean did someone ask you?" Jane was looking around, bewildered.

"No, I'm just going to ask that guy over there in the red sweater. I saw him dancing before and he's pretty good. Don't want to get stuck with a 'Bob and Floater.'"

"What's that?" Jane asked.

"You know. Those guys who close their eyes real goonylike and just sort of bob and float around the floor and think they're dancing."

She saw Jane write down "Bob and Floater," before she looked up and pressed Andy with another question.

"But aren't you supposed to wait until some guy asks *you* to dance?"

"Oh no. This is the modern age. If I waited, I might not get to dance to the numbers I really want to dance to. And then I might get a Bob and Floater, or worse, a 'Mexican Jumping Bean.'"

"I can guess what *they* dance like," Jane said, taking the note down in her book. "Well, this is very interesting, I must say. You don't mind if I watch, do you?"

"Not at all," Andy said. "Be my guest." She

was halfway across the floor, when she turned and came back to where Jane was standing. "You'll probably be wondering what the secret of my success is, what I'm saying to this guy, so I'll tell you now."

"Yes?" Jane said curiously.

"I'll be saying, 'Want to dance?' "

Jane, of course, wrote it down.

Then she watched as Andy strolled casually across the dance floor, which was bathed in light that changed from red to blue to green, and walked up to the designated guy in the red sweater and, about two seconds later, came back out onto the dance floor with him.

Jane watched Andy admiringly. She didn't know much about this kind of dancing, but she'd seen enough dance performances to know when someone used space well, and Andy really did. She was completely unself-conscious, perfectly synchronized with the beat. The guy she was with wasn't quite as good, but he was working to keep up with her.

Jane turned her attention to the other couples on the floor and saw what Andy meant about "Bob and Floaters" and "Mexican Jumping Beans." She even came up with a few other categories, including the "Living Deads" and the "Think They're Doing It Rights." There wasn't anyone on the floor as good as Andy. Apparently that fact was clear to the Oakley guys, too, as three of them in a row asked Andy to dance.

When she'd taken notes on the dancers,

Jane shifted her attention to the band.

Ugh, what a scruffy bunch, she thought, but figured she'd have to get closer to take down notes on what they looked like. And so she moved up close to the stage and began doing little written sketches of each member of the group.

The drummer was a heavyset guy wearing a baseball cap and a tank T-shirt in fluorescent green. The keyboard player was a six-foot-tall beanpole in a pink tuxedo jacket and Hawaiian print pants. The bass guitar player looked like a relatively normal human being to Jane. He had short hair and was wearing plain khaki pants and a navy polo shirt. Then she moved her gaze to the lead guitarist. If the bass player was normal, this guy was the exact opposite. Everything about him was strange.

First there was his hair, which was not as long as Jane's, but longer than the hair on any boy she knew. The color was somewhere between blond and brown. She couldn't tell what color his eyes were because he was wearing tiny horn-rim sunglasses. He had on black jeans and little black boots with folded-over tops and pointy toes and a white T-shirt and a black leather jacket. But by far the most amazing thing about him was the single silver stud earring he had in one ear. She had to admit he sang well, although not in a style she liked. He had a reedy, raspy voice and sang with what sounded like a lot of feeling.

Jane wrote all of this down. He would make quite an interesting character in her paper. When she was through, she looked up at him to make sure she'd gotten everything into her notes. To her astonishment, he was looking straight back at her, holding the gaze as he sang, as if he was singing to her. Then, worse, he began laughing at her. Unfortunately, she was close enough to the stage for him to bend over while he was playing and shout down at her, "You writing my biography? I'd like to read it."

She quickly slapped her notepad shut and moved away from the stage. With all the dignity she could muster, she forced herself not to run into the ladies' room, but to calmly walk around the edge of the crowd until she got to the back wall of the gym, into the darkness beyond all the lights that were streaming down on him and the rest of the group.

From this vantage point, she could watch this dreadful person without any risk of him watching her back. And he really was dreadful, she decided. So scruffy-looking and at the same time so arrogant about how he looked. She'd heard how rock stars were so infatuated with themselves, and here was living proof. She shuddered when the thought occurred to her that he had probably thought she was gawking at him because she thought he was *attractive*! The nerve!

She couldn't help comparing him to Neal. They really were total opposites. Neal was so

tall and clean-cut, and had such an open smile.
This guy was so small and wiry, and when
he'd laughed at her it was with a kind of
smugness. As if he knew her, but she didn't
know him.

She watched him, just to reconfirm how
much she disliked him, through the last two
songs of the set. And then the lights went dark
on the stage and the band shut down, and the
awful guy propped his guitar against one of
the amps, and ambled off for a break.

Jane scanned the crowd for Andy, spotted
her in the middle of the dance floor. It looked
like she was showing a couple of guys how to
do a routine of steps. Jane was amazed at how
easily Andy seemed to glide into the social
situation here. Jane did all right on this
score, but not much better than all right. She
had a few good friends, mostly girls like herself. And she had Neal. She'd been glad all
last year that she had a boyfriend back home.
It saved her from having to come to dances
like this, and pancake breakfasts, and fall leaf
rakes — just to meet guys. She was all set. It
made life so much easier, she thought, being
all set.

She wasn't quite sure what she should do
during this little break. She wanted to really
take in the full scene so when she started to
write about it tomorrow, she'd have all her
impressions at hand to draw from.

She decided to head for the girls' bathroom
and hang out by the mirrors, listening to the

comments about the evening. That way, she could incorporate actual quotes into her paper.

She turned and started to walk in that direction, and then felt a hand on her shoulder.

"Can I see what you wrote about me?" a soft voice said.

She turned to see the lead singer of Ambulance. And he was smiling that same infuriating, all-knowing smile at her.

"What makes you think it was about you?" she asked haughtily, shrugging his hand away, starting again toward the hallway where the ladies' room was.

"Come on," he said, now walking beside her. "Don't lie. Just tell me why you're doing all this writing, instead of dancing like everyone else."

Jane sighed loudly so he'd know she found him extremely tiresome, then said, "Not that it's any of your business, but I'm recording a strange and exotic experience for a creative writing assignment."

"A dance is a strange and exotic experience?" he said. "Exactly what planet do you come from? I know!" He pointed in mock recognition. "You're that new exchange student from Pluto."

"Very funny," she said sarcastically and kept walking. She wasn't surprised that he was so rude. What else could she expect from a conceited rock singer? She wondered if he got away with talking like this to other girls. Probably. They probably all swooned in front of the stage when he sang and played, and then died of ecstasy if he talked to them. Well, he had a surprise coming if he was expecting that kind of interest from her.

"Hey," he said now, "I'm sorry. Don't take me seriously."

"Oh," she said, looking straight at him, "believe me, I don't."

"Ouch!" he cried, clutching at his chest as if she'd actually wounded him. Then he got serious. "Please. I'm really interested. Most kids I know *live* at dances and rock concerts. It's kind of their goldfish bowl. I've never met anyone who'd think *this* was a strange place. What's a nonstrange place to you?"

"Oh, I don't know. An art museum. A modern dance performance. The library."

He ran a hand through his hair, which was tangled, probably from all the throwing himself around that he did on stage.

"Well, I've been in those places, so I guess we're ,not totally from different solar systems."

"*You've* been at dance performances and in museums?"

"Oh yeah, I've probably been everywhere you've been. I just kind of left it all behind a while back. But before I was here, I was where you are. I was very Boston proper, just like you."

Jane was indignant. How dare this guy in

long hair and leather jacket and earring tell her he'd left *her* world behind?

Now he was peering at her. Finally he said, "I think I even recognize you a little. Didn't you go to Miss Haversham's grammar school?"

"You know Miss Haversham's?"

"Mmmhmm. I went to Pine Grove. I think you were in that little Thursday afternoon ballroom dance class all our mothers sent us to."

"The Fortnightlies? With Mrs. Nunnely? But I don't remember you."

He smiled and said, "I weighed about sixty pounds then and had hideous zits. I was probably the kid you were trying desperately to avoid having to dance with."

It was her turn to peer hard at him. Then she said, "I think I *did* have to dance with you. The cha cha. Everyone else had already chosen up partners and so Mrs. Nunnelly just pushed us together. No one wanted to be my partner then, either. I had braces and those awful rubber bands that kept popping out of my mouth all the time."

She stopped, realizing that she was having an actual conversation with this stuck-on-himself, minor-league rock star. But he didn't seem so conceited anymore. "What's your name?"

"Cary Slade," he said.

"Jane Barrett," she said, then got stuck in her confusion over him. Suddenly she couldn't think of anything to say. She didn't have to as it turned out. Belinda Miller, who was both the most beautiful *and* the smartest girl in the junior class, was suddenly at Cary Slade's side, linking her arm through his, tugging at him.

"Come on," she said. "Buy me a Coke, and then I'll tell you how great you were up there tonight."

"Guess I can't turn that down," he said, taking Belinda's hand. Then, when the two of them had started off toward the hall, he turned, as if giving Jane an afterthought, and said, "Good luck with your paper! I'll try to get the guys to play a cha cha and dedicate it to you."

Jane felt her cheeks flare. Was he teasing, or just making fun of her? Probably making fun. He doubtless thought she was just another snobby Back Bay girl. Boston proper as he'd put it. He thought he knew her without knowing her, that she was just a type he'd gotten beyond. Now he was with Belinda Miller. Belinda was a superstar. Jane was just a girl who had once had braces.

In spite of her usually reserved manner, Jane felt a thin trickle of tears beginning to run down her cheeks. She ran for the nearest exit. She knew she shouldn't be going back to school alone. It was a rule. You didn't walk on country roads by yourself. You had to be with at least one other girl. But Jane didn't care about rules at the moment.

Outside, she caught her breath, and wiped her eyes, and started walking home, angrily kicking through every pile of leaves on the way. This was exactly the reason she was lucky to already have a perfectly good boyfriend back home. If you didn't, you just wound up going to things like this where you met guys you hated and then were crushed when they didn't like you.

Chapter Eleven

Dad,
How's Max? Does he miss me? Are you making sure to add the antibiotic to his feed for that barb wire cut in his leg? And did you get the strays rounded up and the fence mended out in Palmer's pasture? Have you had any more hail storms?

I miss everything about back there. I hate it here. Truly. I tried to like it for a day and I still hated it, so I know I really hate it. I feel like a chicken in a coop. I'm in this one room with two other girls. One is from Chicago and talks more than everybody in Rattlesnake Creek put together. She's nice, but I don't know how to edge in with my one or two words in the middle of her hundreds. The other girl is from Boston and is kind of stuck up. I think she thinks I'm some kind of wild coyote just in from the desert. Looks at me sideways now and then, as if she's trying to figure if I'm going to bite.

They are both off to some dumb dance tonight. I am staying here listening to the one country station they've got on the radio. It tears me up to listen to all these songs about where I want to be.

The classes here are hard, but I'm trying to keep up. I'm not going to make you ashamed of me. The food here is worse than at Lula's Lunch. I can see you saying "impossible" but it's true. They've got stuff no one can say for sure what it is. Not even the girls dishing it up.

I've made one friend. Well really about half a friend as I'm not sure he thinks that much of me. His name is Randy Crowell and his people run a horse farm out this way. He lets me ride, although — like you — he thinks I'm a darn fool on a horse. He doesn't talk much. I like being with him but can't at all figure out why.

I'm not getting into any mischief. Don't really have the spirit for it. I am feeling pretty full of woe. Maybe you would reconsider and let me come home.

Yr daughter,
October

P.S. Check in on Pumpkin for me, will you? I think she's meaning to have those kittens of hers up in the hayloft.

CHAPTER TWELVE

Saturday morning came up sunny, but with an edge of coolness to it. Fall was moving in on this part of Massachusetts.

Jane sat on the old slatted wooden bench outside the white frame building that served as the Greenleaf train depot. She had only worn a sweater and jeans, and in the shade it was a little chilly. She wrapped her arms around herself. She was deep in thought. What she was trying to do was remember her boyfriend Neal, who was due in on the train from Boston in a few minutes.

It was ridiculous, really. She had known him practically all her life, and she had only been away from him for one week. And it wasn't as if she *completely* couldn't remember him, like those people in movies who have amnesia and can't remember their families or job or what state they're living in or what year it is. It wasn't like that.

She could remember perfectly well the color of Neal's eyes and his height, and she knew before the train even got in what color his jacket would be. He'd be wearing a tweed sportjacket with a wool scarf around his neck. Through all but the worst of the winter, he'd wear this same jacket, only with a scarf wound around his neck. The guys at his prep school all did this. If you wore a heavy jacket, you were a wimp. Jane thought this was one of the stupidest traditions she'd ever heard of.

So she knew what he'd be wearing, and she knew he'd gotten his hair cut this week. If she was a witness to a crime and Neal was the criminal, she could give the police a perfect description of him. But still, when she closed her eyes and tried to imagine him, she couldn't quite pull him into focus.

This was a little unsettling. Even more unsettling was the fact that, every time she scrunched up her mind and tried to think only of Neal, she could only hold onto the thought for a little while before other thoughts came creeping in. Specifically, thoughts of Cary Slade — whom she could see so sharply in every detail that it was as if his image had been etched into her mind.

She wasn't sure what this was about. Probably she was still stinging from the humiliation of last night. She kept thinking that if Cary Slade really knew her, he wouldn't be so quick to dismiss her as just another typical Boston Back Bay girl. If he knew about the stories she wrote, which she thought were quite sensitive and perceptive about life. . . . If he knew that she sang, that she and her older sister Charlotte organized a choral group every Christmas to sing in twenty different homes for the elderly. . . . If he knew that she really preferred sweat pants and sweat shirts to fancy clothes. . . . If. . . .

But why did she even *care* what he thought about her? Why was she worried about the opinion of some scruffy guy who wore sunglasses at night and thought playing an electric guitar made him a big star? Why was she concerned about someone who thought the way they'd grown up was stupid when she thought it was pretty neat? And why did she keep thinking about the way he looked in that black leather jacket, wondering if he had a motorcycle to go with it? She'd never been on a motorcycle in her life, had never wanted to. She thought they were noisy and dangerous. Cars were so much nicer and more tasteful. When Neal took her out, it was in his father's BMW — a civilized way to travel.

Everything about Neal was civilized. There were never any unpleasant surprises about him. He was always, well always just Neal. And soon he'd be hopping off the train and she wouldn't have to try to pull him into focus. He'd be there and smiling, and he'd give her one of his great hugs, and he'd be full of news from home. And all these distract-

ing and disturbing thoughts of Cary Slade
would vanish, as she and Neal set off on the
Saturday they'd been planning all week.

But it didn't quite work out that way. The
train was an hour late. By the time it pulled
up to the depot, Jane was furious with the
railroad, and a little put out with Neal for taking the train instead of just borrowing his
dad's car.

Neal got off the train looking rumpled and
tired. One side of his face was full of little red
dots, she guessed from where he'd fallen asleep
against the old velvet upholstery of the train
seat. He seemed glad to see her, but not quite
as glad as she'd been expecting. He gave her
only a quick hug and then was looking
around.

"We won the race," he said, "and then
really partied afterward. I didn't get in until
late. And then had to get up at six to make
the train. And I still haven't had a cup of
coffee. Is there any place around where I can
get one?"

Jane nodded toward the Greaf Diner, across
the street from the train depot. At one time
it had been the Greenleaf Diner, but so many
of the middle letters had long ago burnt out
and never been replaced that everyone had
just come to call it by what letters it had left
— Greaf.

Although there were a lot of Canby Hall

girls who met there for burgers and Cokes in the late afternoon, Jane had never been inside the Greaf. She walked over with Neal, looking hard at his face so she wouldn't forget even the slightest bit of it again. Now that she was looking at it, she couldn't imagine why she hadn't been able to see it in her mind's eye. It was the same face she'd been looking at since the early days of grade school. Maybe that was the problem. Maybe she'd been looking at Neal for so long that she'd stopped really *seeing* him.

She pulled open the door of the diner and let Neal go through ahead of her. She'd broken him of the habit of trying to open doors for her a couple of years ago. She considered herself a feminist and didn't think feminists ought to stand around looking helpless while their boyfriends opened doors for them.

Inside the diner, it was cool and dark. There was a long counter with maybe twenty stools and along the wall a few booths. In the back there was a huge jukebox. Nothing was playing on it now. It was quiet in the diner. There were only half a dozen customers, eating late breakfasts or early lunches. A blackboard announced that Today's Special was Meatloaf & Mashed Pot. w/ Veg. There were also pieces of pie on display on shelves in glass cases on the counter. Jane took all this in before she noticed the by far most interesting feature of the Greaf Diner, which was that the counterman was Cary Slade.

She actually blinked hard when she finally did see him — as if he were a product of her imagination and she could blink him away. But he stayed right there where he was, looking straight at her and Neal, and smiling that knowing smile of his.

She looked at Neal and thought she knew what Cary Slade was smiling at. He was thinking that Neal was the typical preppy. Short hair, and tweed jacket, and jeans with a crease, and unironed oxford cloth shirt with a casually wrinkled tie.

Then she felt crummy for knowing why Cary was smiling. In a way, it put her in on his joke, put her in league with him, against Neal. She didn't want to do this, and so she decided the best thing was to be cool to Cary.

"Oh," she said. "Hi." And then took a stool at the counter, quickly grabbed a plastic-enclosed menu, and fixed her gaze on the list of breakfast combinations.

Neal hailed Cary with a raised hand and said, "Can we have a couple of cups of coffee over here?"

"Yes sir!" Cary said, leaping over to the coffee pots. "Coming right up!"

Neal didn't catch his sarcasm, just scanned the menu. Neal's family was hugely wealthy. They had a full-time, live-in maid and cook at their house, and so Neal was used to being waited on, and to not noticing the people who were doing the waiting.

Cary Slade was not, however, about to be ignored. At least not by Jane. "Did you get the story you wanted last night?" he asked her casually as he was filling their cups.

Neal looked up from his menu, surprised.

"Uh, more or less, thank you," Jane said, trying to make it sound like he was someone who had asked her for directions on the street. Of course she'd still have to explain Cary to Neal, and from the curiosity on Neal's face, it looked like it had better be now.

"This is the guitar player in the band that played at the dance last night," she said to Neal, then to Cary, "I'm sorry. I forgot your name."

It was a lie, but it seemed to fool both guys.

"That's okay," Cary said, not offering his name, though.

"He gave me some professional background on rock and roll," she lied again, and this one also sailed by.

"Yeah, well, if you need any more, uh, any more background for that story, well, you know where to find me," Cary said.

Jane rushed in with a change of subject. "I am *starving*. I think I'm going to have the Paul Bunyan Special," she said, slapping her menu closed.

"You sure?" Cary said, taking out a little green order pad. "We've had some lumberjacks couldn't polish that one off. You might want to try the Good Morning Special instead."

"Nope. Bring on the Paul Bunyan. When I'm hungry I could eat a whole cow."

"That's good," Cary said, "because there's a side dish of whole cow that comes with the Paul Bunyan. Not to mention the silo of toast."

In spite of herself, Jane found this incredibly funny, and started getting The Giggles. For her, The Giggles were an unstoppable force. If she got them, there was no use trying to suppress them. The only thing was to go with them. Which didn't keep her from feeling stupid the whole time she was laughing. It hadn't been *that* funny a joke.

Cary was clearly pleased that she found him to be such a great wit. He took Neal's order while Jane was still shaking with internal chuckles. Then, as he was sticking his order pencil behind his ear, he winked at her and walked off to the window to the kitchen, where he put the order ticket in a clip on a revolving stand for the cook.

"So you had a good time last night," Neal said, after dumping three packets of sugar into his coffee and enough cream to make it beige. Jane had always found this habit cute. This morning, it seemed a little sickening.

"Oh, I don't know. It was pretty childish — everybody hopping around to loud music.

Give me a chamber music concert any day. But I think I got enough to write a good paper."

"Well, I guess you might say *we* acted pretty childish last night," he said, smiling at the memory. "You know. After the race. Winners night out."

"I'm glad to hear the Rep Tie won," she said. That was the name of the sailboat Neal crewed on. Rep ties were the striped ties prep school guys wore with their uniform blazers.

"And it was the roughest race of the season. We had the trickiest winds this side of a monsoon. Had to tack most of the way. There we were, just round the first buoy and Kip said. . . ."

He was off into a sailing story. Jane nearly always tuned out when he launched into them. She had no interest in sailing, and so she just tried to look interested, and nod, and make appreciative sounds at the right places in the story, while thinking her own thoughts. She'd done this forever and hadn't felt bad about it until today. Of course in the past her other thoughts were about conjugations of French verbs, or the play she and Charlotte had gone to see the night before. Today the thoughts were about the Greaf Diner's counterman who, Jane could see out of the corner of her eye, was standing down at the end of the counter, leaning against the wall, reading a paperback book. But not really. At least in the instant she allowed herself to really look at him, he was looking above the top of the book, straight at her. And he smiled. And this time there was no smirk in it.

Cary broke away from this moment of eye contact, got their breakfasts, and brought them over. By now, Jane was way too unsettled to be hungry and so left most of the Paul Bunyan Special. Neal commented on this.

"Odd. I don't think I've ever seen you not hungry."

"I guess my eyes were bigger than my stomach when I ordered," she said, watching Neal devour his Sunny-Side-Up Special.

When they were finished, Cary came over and put the green check face down in front of Jane. She saw instantly that he'd written something on the back, and knew it probably wasn't "Have a nice day. Your waiter, Cary." She picked it up quickly and fished her wallet out of her backpack.

"My treat," she told Neal. "I'll pay up at the cash register." On the way, she glanced down at what was scrawled on the check. It read:

I think we already know each other. And I think I'd like to know you even better.

In spite of herself, in spite of thinking she didn't know Cary Slade at all and probably wouldn't like him if she did; in spite of for several years now not having had a single thought of another boy besides Neal; in spite of feeling she was betraying someone she cared about, she found herself handing the check across the register to Cary Slade and nodding ever so slightly at him to show him she agreed with the message.

She looked at Neal who, much to Jane's relief, hadn't noticed anything.

CHAPTER THIRTEEN

From breakfast, Jane and Neal went for a long walk in the hilly country around Greenleaf. She told him everything that had been going on this first week (well, everything except her confusing thoughts about Cary Slade), and he was sympathetic, as he always was. And when he told her about *his* week — about the pipe breaking in one of the washrooms at his school, flooding nearly the whole first floor; about the fight he'd had with his brother Josh — Jane was interested, as usual. But she could see now that it was more a friendly interest than a romantic one. Neal was her best friend, she knew that for sure. But did she really feel toward him like you were supposed to feel toward your boyfriend?

Later that night they were sitting up in the balcony of the Bijou Theater in Greenleaf, watching a new Richard Gere movie. During the big love scene, Neal tightened his arm

around Jane's shoulder and leaned over to
kiss her cheek.

She could remember when it sent chills and
thrills through her. But this time something
new happened. After Neal had kissed her and
they had both settled back in their seats and
were eating popcorn and watching the movie,
Jane found herself still thinking about kissing. But not about kissing Neal. She found
herself imagining what it would be like to
kiss Cary Slade.

At nine, when he had walked her back to
Baker, before catching the last train to Boston, Jane gave Neal an especially big hug at
the door, to make up for the thoughts he
didn't even know she'd been having.

I'm being ridiculous, she thought. Neal has
always been my one true love and he always
will be. This way I'm feeling lately is just a
passing phase. I'll snap back by next weekend.

And as she watched him walk away into the
night, she almost believed herself.

Jane carried this tumble of thoughts up the
old marble stairs to the fourth floor corridor.
As she pushed open the door onto the low-lit
hall, she heard all the cozy sounds of laughter
and music and cards slapping onto desk tops.
Hearts was the big game in Baker and Saturday nights were "Hearts Mania" time for girls
in for the evening. She felt sad coming into all

this, knowing that she'd find none of this fun going on in 407.

But she was wrong. Both her roommates were not only in the room, but awake and actually talking to each other! Something was definitely up.

Andy seemed upset, agitated. She was pacing up and down the length of the room. She was muttering, whether to Toby or to herself, Jane couldn't tell at first. Toby was flustered, fixing a mug of something with Andy's little immersion heater stick. She brought it over to Andy and made her sit down at her desk with it. Then Toby turned and noticed Jane standing in the doorway.

"I made her some hot cocoa," she said to Jane. "My Dad always fixes me some when I'm upset." Then she shrugged to show she thought it was probably not enough.

"What's wrong?" Jane asked.

Andy turned and jumped up from her desk and threw her hands up in the air and shouted, "What's wrong? You won't believe it when I tell you. It's my family. Every day they call, and every day I tell them I'm just fine and dandy here. And then they call the next day and ask the same thing. Well, tonight they called and said they're not sure they really believe me. They say there's something sad in my voice. And so they're driving out here next weekend to make sure with their own eyes. Argh! You'd think I'd been kidnapped by some weirdo cult or something, not just at a nice safe boarding school."

"But you're *not* completely happy. Things haven't been so great in this room, and they've probably picked up on it," Toby said, surprising the other two. It was about the most she'd said at one time since she'd arrived.

Andy sat back down again and nodded slowly, thinking about this. And then she went from nodding to shaking her head from side to side. And then she began softly crying.

"I knew cocoa wouldn't do it," Toby said fretfully, pulling up a chair next to Andy.

"But *we* can do something to help," Jane said, coming all the way into the room, peeling off her navy blazer, and dropping it on the floor (which ordinarily would have driven Andy crazy, but which she didn't even notice at the moment). She sat down on the bed next to Andy. She reached a hand out toward Toby, who got the message, pulled a Kleenex from the box on her desk, and handed it to Jane, who passed it on to Andy.

This gesture of kindness, unfortunately, only made Andy cry all the harder. The other two waited her out, until she was down to just sniffling. She looked over at Jane, dabbed at her nose, and asked, "How can you help?"

"Well, we can give them what they want. We can show them how happy you are here at Canby Hall, especially in this cocoon of warmth and friendship, this family away from home — dear old 407."

"You're being sarcastic," Andy said, sniffling some more.

"Of course," Jane said. "But they don't have to know that. For two days we can put on the greatest show on campus. We can convince them that everything here's absolutely rosy."

Andy stared at Jane for a long moment, trying to play the scheme through in her mind, trying to imagine it working.

"Maybe," she finally admitted. "But would you two really be willing to go through with it?"

Jane nodded and said, "Of course. I know you really want to stay here. If you want to try this, you've got me one-hundred percent. For two days I'll be the most devoted and loving roommate you've ever seen. And I'm quite a good actress when I put my mind to it. I was a wise man in three Christmas pageants and I played a tree in *The Little Forest*. I never let my branches droop once."

"But what about you, October?" Andy asked.

"I don't know. I'd try for sure, but I've never done any playacting. Maybe I'd mess it up for you."

"Oh, don't worry about that," Jane told her. "We'll work out the whole plan ahead of time, so you'll know exactly what to do."

"Oh, you guys," Andy said, sighing, "this is so great of you. But we've got to start brainstorming right away. There's so much to plan.

When they roll through those Canby Hall gates on Friday, I want us to be perfect."

"We can start tonight," Jane said. "Is that a notepad you have on your desk there, October? Let's start making a list."

"Oh, how nice," Andy said. "A conspiracy. And I've got two co-conspirators." She rubbed her hands in glee.

And the three of them began plotting, going on with this until after one in the morning. When they were through, and Andy was down in the lavatory, brushing her teeth before bed, Maggie Morrison came in from a big game of Hearts that was still going on in her room from the sound of it.

"Got to put in my night retainer," she said, standing in front of the mirror next to the one Andy was using. "I can't wait until I finally get these braces off. I've completely forgotten what my teeth look like. Maybe they're not even in there anymore. Oh, hey. I was looking for you earlier. Dana called me today on the WATS line from our Dad's office, so we got to talk a while. I mentioned the trouble in 407 and she had some advice."

Andy nodded and said, through the toothpaste and brush, "Shoot."

"Well, she said she thought it would help if the three of you could find some group activity you could get into together."

"We sort of figured that out ourselves. I think we've got something."

"What did you come up with?" Maggie

asked. "A sport? A game? Have you started playing Hearts?"

"No, we decided a nice conspiracy was what we needed."

Maggie gave Andy a question mark look in the mirror.

"I'll tell you tomorrow. It's too late now," Andy said, and walked out of the washroom and down the hall, for the first time happy to be heading back to 407.

CHAPTER FOURTEEN

Sunday night, Dee threw a surfing party in the fourth floor lavatory. She invited everyone on the hall. Andrea, who loved parties, was delighted to go. Toby, who was shy and had little experience with social events of any kind, would much rather have just crawled under her blanket and hid out for the rest of the night. But Dee was really her only friend on campus and she didn't want to insult her. Jane thought the whole idea sounded foolish and so begged off, saying she had to work on her creative writing assignment. Which she did.

By the time Andy put on her swim suit and got Toby reluctantly in tow (wearing her school-issue, 1950s-style tank suit from home), the party was in full swing. Beach towels were spread out all over the floor, with girls all over them — either sitting and gossiping and munching on snacks, or up and dancing around. Dee had talked everyone into bringing their best goodies — candy and chips and cans of bean dip — and their radios. Everyone tuned them to the same rock station, so the sound reverberating off the high tile walls was loud. Dee had also collected all the desk lamps on the floor and positioned them around to create the effect of a beach at high noon.

The surfing was being done in the shower room, where all the spigots were going full blast. Dee and Maggie had brought over all the floor mats from the gym and put them both on the floor, and around the walls as buffers. Then they had dumped a couple of bottles of liquid detergent on them and turned on the water. It was a melee of squealing girls in there, some surfing on their feet, most though, doing stomach sliders across the mats.

Dee wasn't fooled though, not even by her own tricks, and told Toby she thought maybe she was only making herself more depressed with this party.

"No, it's great," Toby tried to cheer her up. "You've really got the surfing spirit going here."

"How would you know?" Dee said, looking depressed. "You live in a desert."

"I saw all those old *Gidget* movies on tv," Toby said. "This party really reminds me of them."

"It does?" Dee said.

"Well, not really," said Toby, who never could follow through with a lie. "But everyone's still having a lot of fun."

"Except me," Dee said glumly.

"Why don't we go to the ocean?" Toby said. "Maybe that would really make you feel better. I hear they have one around here."

Dee looked at Toby hard, trying to figure out if she was being serious. Sometimes it was hard to tell.

"But it's not the same as *my* ocean," Dee said.

"Still, it must have waves."

"Wimpy ones, I hear."

"Let's go check them out, anyway," Toby said. "And soon. Before you know it, it's going to be winter. The first real winter you and I will ever have been through."

"You really want to do this?"

"Sure," Toby said.

"Next weekend?"

"Great," Toby started to say, then stopped herself, snapping her fingers. "I forgot. Next weekend there's this big crisis we've got to deal with. Andy's family is driving out from Chicago to rescue her from this awful place. We have to put on this big act to convince them that she's the happiest girl at Canby Hall and we're the happiest room on campus."

"Wow," Dee said, drifting into her own thoughts, "imagine having your family coming to save you from this place. Do you think they'd take *us* back with them instead?"

Both girls grinned wryly, then Dee hopped off the sink she was sitting on and gave Toby a pat on the shoulder.

"Well, my dear, I really have to be going now. I must mingle with my guests, you see. Oh," she said, putting a hand dramatically to her heart, "the duties of a hostess!"

Toby watched her leave, and settled back, leaning against a mirror, not minding being a wallflower, watching everybody else.

Meanwhile, Maggie had left to find Jane. She'd been counting on this party as an opportunity to talk with Jane, maybe draw her out on the problems in 407. But she was nowhere to be seen.

She found her alone in her room at her desk, bent over a small electronic typewriter, her feet awash in crumbled up wads of typing paper. She was staring off into space and didn't seem to hear Maggie come in.

"Hi," Maggie said, and introduced herself. "I hope the party's not distracting you too much."

"Well, it *is* a bit of an annoyance," Jane admitted. "Maybe you could close the door."

"Behind me as I leave?" Maggie asked

Jane smiled. "I see I'm getting a reputation as a wet blanket around here. No, come in."

Maggie nodded, and then asked what Jane was working on.

"Oh, it's this creative writing assignment. I've got to describe this awful dance I went to Friday night and —"

She was interrupted by the phone ringing.

"Excuse me," she said to Maggie as she went over, picked it up, and said hello into the receiver.

"Hi," said a strangely familiar male voice on the other end of the line. "I was wondering if you needed the services of an expert consultant on the subject of rock and roll."

"Oh, uh, well, no thanks. I've really got the paper nearly done," Jane lied, not knowing what to say, not wanting to have this conversation with Maggie in the room overhearing it.

"Well then, if you've got your paper done, and your boyfriend packed off to Boston — I saw him out the window of the diner last night waiting for the Late Express — then you've probably got time to go out and grab a pizza with me."

He was so sure of himself, so arrogant, Jane thought. How dare he assume she was interested in him?

"No, thank you. I'm enjoying having a quiet night here. Good-bye." She hung up and turned to Maggie and said, as if the phone call hadn't taken place, "So how is your sister Dana?"

Jane listened as Maggie detailed her sister's life in Hawaii, but try as she would to keep her mind on this conversation, Jane kept finding herself distracted by thoughts of Cary Slade.

The party, with its swells of laughter and shouting, and its constant surge of rock music, provided a backdrop to Maggie. But then all of a sudden, it seemed as though the music doubled in volume or amplitude or something.

"Boy," Jane said, "I guess the party's really getting into gear. It sounds like they turned all the radios up at once, and switched half of them to another station."

Maggie cocked an ear toward the hallway, then after a moment said, "I don't think all that music's coming from the party."

The two of them became silent again, trying to figure out where the additional sound was coming from. In this stillness, they both became aware that it was a single voice, a male voice. And after another few moments' listening, they began to make out words:

Hey Jane Jane Jane
Can you come out and play?
Can you let down your hair,
Or will you stay up there in your tower?

"Oh no!" Jane cried out and ran to the window, throwing it open and sticking her head out. There, down on the front lawn of Baker, stood Cary Slade with his guitar and amp. He smiled up when he saw her, but kept on singing. It was a James Taylor-type ballad, with lyrics apparently written especially for the occasion.

Hey Jane Jane Jane.
What's this game we're playin'?
How come you're not sayin'
What you really mean?

He paused after this verse and shouted up to her, "So. You want to come have some pizza with me, or should I go on with the song? I should warn you that it only gets worse from here. And," he said, waving a hand to indicate the Baker windows facing the lawn, "we seem to be drawing quite a crowd."

Jane could see that Maggie was at the other window. And who knew how many other Baker girls were witnessing this little scene? She was mortified. Surely she looked like a fool with this weird guy standing down there, his guitar plugged into the outside utility jack, wailing away like some demented serenader in old Spain. Madcap guys weren't anything Jane had any experience with. She was used to Neal, who was always the model of decorum. He'd *never* do anything like this.

Maybe that's why you're bored with him, a voice from somewhere deep inside Jane said. She quickly pushed the traitorous thought away. Then she looked back down at Cary Slade, who was threatening to launch into yet another verse.

"No, no!" she shouted down to him. "I'll come. It's blackmail, but I'll do it. Give me five minutes to find my shoes."

"Friend of yours?" Maggie said innocently, when the two of them had pulled themselves back into the room.

"I don't even *know* the guy!" Jane said indignantly.

"Sure seems like a pretty intense drama for two people who don't even know each other."

"Well, the truth is I met him at the dance on Friday night. He seems to think that I like him, when actually I find him quite annoying."

"But you're going out with him for pizza, anyway."

"Well, if I don't, he's just going to keep bellowing out there like some cat on an ashcan. I'm not really feeling up to that much embarrassment."

As Jane began getting ready — changing her whole outfit, not just her shoes — Maggie got up to leave.

"Well," she said, "nobody asked my opinion, but I'll give it, anyway. *I* think he's kind of cute. Don't you — really?"

Jane turned and looked at Maggie and said, "Oh, yeah, about as cute as your average cobra."

By the time Jane got downstairs, Cary had packed his guitar and amp into the back of his tiny Honda and was leaning against it, arms folded across his chest, feet crossed at the ankles, in a waiting posture.

"All right," she said huffily, "you've got me down here. We might as well get going."

"Oh no," Cary said, unfolding himself, coming over to her. He took her two arms by the elbows and looked her in the eyes. "I'm not dragging you off if you don't want to go. This isn't a kidnapping. If you don't want to see me, I'll get in my car and drive off and not bother you again. But I'm hoping you'll give me a chance. Just a little one. So, what'll it be? Which box are you going to check — Yes or No?"

Jane looked at him and sighed. "Yes . . ."

He started to move toward the car, but she stopped him by putting her hand on his arm. ". . . *if* you take off those sunglasses."

"Oh no!" he wailed, grinning. "Not my shades. Stripped of my greatest defense! You'll be able to see through all my wiles."

"Good," Jane said, picking the glasses off the bridge of his nose, folding them, and slipping them into the pocket of her blazer. "I'll just hold onto them until you bring me back here."

She went around and got in the passenger side. He started up the Honda and they were off toward Greenleaf.

"I want you to hear something," he said, and pressed the PLAY button on the tape deck in the dashboard. Instantly, the car was filled with a kind of music Jane had never heard before — tricky, sophisticated piano playing, but not classical. Modern, but not rock. She listened for a long time, then turned to Cary.

"It's wonderful," she said. "What is it?"

"Keith Jarrett."

"Playing or composing?" she asked.

"Both," Cary said. "The guy's a genius."

"I've never heard anything quite like it," she admitted.

"I went through all my tapes tonight to try to find something to move you closer to rock and roll."

She was totally surprised. "But why?" she asked. "Why would you care what I think about your music?"

"Oh, I don't know. I guess I'm just a missionary at heart. Looking for converts wherever I can find them."

Jane felt a slight thud in her heart, realizing this probably meant he didn't care about her specifically — just about his music.

They had driven into Greenleaf by now and were pulling up in front of Pizza Pete's. When he'd parked and turned off the ignition, he said, "I wasn't quite telling the truth back there." He looked down at the steering wheel as he spoke. "It wasn't just about getting someone to like my music. It was about getting *you* to like it. Which I guess is part of wanting *you* to like *me*."

"Why do you care if I like you? You keep acting like you already know me, anyway.

You know — typical Boston predebutante. So what's the point?"

"Well," he said now, turning to look at her. With his glasses off, she could see his eyes, which were blue and truthful. "I guess part of it is that I *do* sort of feel like I know you. Sort of like we're old friends who've just met. But there's also something different about you — different from other girls I've met."

"Oh, I can't be as different as Belinda," Jane said, not fishing for a compliment, just being honest.

"Belinda's my best friend, but she's in love with someone else. She's not my true love. I don't seem to have one of those. What about you? What about the guy you were with in the diner?"

"He's . . . he's an old friend," Jane said tensely. "We've known each other since fourth grade." That's not a lie, Jane thought. We *are* old friends. And we *have* known each other since fourth grade. But what about the *whole* truth? she also thought, but pushed that thought away.

Although it was Sunday night, generally a crowded time at Pizza Pete's, Jane and Cary got lucky and found a booth in the back. He slid in opposite her and folded his arms on the table and smiled, more to himself than at her.

"Penny for your thoughts," she said, truly curious.

"Oh, I charge at least a nickel," he teased.

"Okay then," Jane said, fishing through the side pocket of her jacket, then slapping a nickel on the table between them.

Cary covered it with his hand and said, "I'm just kind of amazed at my luck. I wasn't at all sure I'd get you to come out with me."

She was taken aback. He was not acting at all conceited like she thought he would.

"I'd think you'd be very successful with girls. Big time rock star and all that," she said.

"You'd be surprised if you really knew me. Onstage, I've got this very cool image. I'm above the crowd and there's all the music and lights backing me up, and well, it's kind of like hiding out in this great disguise. Like clowns. Think how much funnier you could be in a clown suit. You could jump around and make a fool of yourself and nobody would know it was really you inside and so you'd have nothing to lose. It's the same thing being in the band. I can smile down at a hundred girls, and be a big heartbreaker with my songs. But put me alone with one girl, and I'm hopeless."

Jane looked across the table at him. She realized that it was really the first time she'd actually done that — *looked* at him. The other times, she'd either been too far away, or too shy, or he'd had those darn glasses on. What she noticed now was how gentle his face was. If you cut his hair, and got rid of the earring and the leather jacket and the glasses, and put him in a flannel shirt and a pair of jeans, he'd really look kind of boyish, like a kid with a paper route. Jane couldn't help smiling at this image.

"Okay," he said, "nickel for your thoughts."

"Oh no," Jane said, laughing. "I charge a *dime* for mine."

He fished one out and slid it across the table toward her.

She didn't tell him about the paper boy image, but she did open up enough to say, "I'm thinking that we *do* have something in common. We both hide behind these images we've set up. You, the rebel, the rock star, the bad boy. Me, the proper, cool, and reserved girl from Boston."

Cary nodded. "You're beginning to see."

"You already figured that out?" Jane said.

"Why do you think I've been chasing you so hard? Did you think I just pack up my guitar and stop at every dorm along the way like some roving minstrel?"

But before Jane had a chance to reply, the waitress was standing over them, tapping her pad impatiently with the tip of her pencil, and they had to come up with their order fast.

"What about pepperoni and black olives?" Cary suggested.

"How did you know that's my favorite?" Jane said, truly amazed.

"I didn't. It's just like I keep trying to tell you. We are kindred souls, Jane Barrett."

CHAPTER FIFTEEN

For the next few days, the three roommates spent every spare minute preparing for Andy's family's visit. Eventually, everyone got into the act. Dee scoured the dorm for stuffed animals to make the place look cozy. Maggie took a heartwarming portrait of the trio and tacked it to the door of 407. Alison was persuaded to volunteer her apartment for a family dinner.

And during this time, all the petty differences, and slights, and small antagonisms that had clouded the atmosphere of 407 utterly evaporated in the hubbub of putting together The Big Plot. It took a lot of planning, but by the time the Cord family's Volvo station wagon pulled through the gates of Canby Hall, "Plan Andrea" was in full readiness.

"They're here!" squealed Andy, who had been sitting in the window seat of 407, on the lookout for the past hour.

"All *right!*" Jane shouted, grabbing Toby by the hand, pulling her off her bed, and out of the room. All three girls rushed down the stairs and out the front door of Baker, arriving on the front steps just as the Cords were emerging from their car. When they spotted Andy, her family swarmed around her, as if she were the winning quarterback after the big game. Neither Toby nor Jane were used to such big displays of family emotion, and so stood slightly off to the side, watching in mild amazement.

As soon as all the kissing and hugging stopped and Andy could get free, she began introductions. "Toby and Jane, I want you to meet my family."

Michael Cord was a tall man with a kind face, a mustache and curly hair all over the sides of his head, but none at all on the top. Andy's older brother Charles looked a lot like his dad, except that he had a lot of hair, worn long and in loose, shiny curls hanging to his collar. Charles was, basically, incredibly handsome.

Andy's younger brother Ted, though, was clearly at his "awkward age." Not only did he have glasses and braces, but he was carrying with him a jar with holes punched in the top and a pet frog inside. Toby's heart went out to him. She could still remember her own pet frog, Hector. She made a mental note to be really interested in Ted's frog.

Jane was fascinated by Andy's mother. She was amazed that a woman with this much activity going on around her, including Baby Nancy wailing away in her car seat, as if she were the Prisoner of Zenda, could remain so cool and composed. Just as Jane was having these thoughts about her, Andy's mother pulled Nancy out of the car seat, turned, and in one swift motion, handed the squalling bundle of flailing arms and legs over to Jane.

"If you wouldn't mind terribly," she said. "I just need to help get a few things out of the back."

And with that she left Jane in an unusual position. Not having any younger brothers or sisters, and never having needed any baby-sitting money, this was the first time in her life she'd ever held a baby. Not that Baby Nancy, despite her name, was exactly a baby anymore. At two, she was a walking, talking, compact mass of energy.

"This is Andrea's friend Jane," Ina Cord said to Baby Nancy, as she walked away. Nancy took a hard look at Jane and then reared her head back. Jane thought she was going to burst into tears, but instead she broke into a hilarious laugh and shouted, "Jujube!"

"No honey." Andy came over and tickled Baby Nancy under her chin. "It's Jane. She's a girl, not a candy."

Baby Nancy appeared to listen to this and

consider it seriously before she nodded and said, seriously, "Jujube."

Everyone laughed, and Charles, with teasing in his eye, added, "Well, I guess that makes you — " he nodded toward Toby " — Totoby."

As shy as Toby was, she had to laugh along with everyone else.

"How did you all like the drive out?" Andy asked.

"Well, this *is* truly beautiful country around here," her father said, folding up his road map, and tossing it through the open car window onto the front seat. "You were right about that. But truthfully, don't you miss the big city way out here?" he asked Andy.

"Well, I did the first day or so, I must admit. But October and Jane were so understanding. Right away, they worked a cure for my homesickness. Come on up to our room and see."

And so they all marched up to 407, which had undergone a major transformation in the past few days. What the Cords saw as they came through the door to the room was a cozy cottage with a decor devoted to Andy's peace of mind. There were the stuffed animals, of course — enough, as Dee had said, "to make a maximum security cell look warm and homey." Also, photos of Chicago were tacked up everywhere — all the city's landmarks. The Hancock Building and the Sears Tower. The Picasso sculpture. Above Andy's bed was a collage of family snapshots, photos of every member of the family.

"We've tried to create a little bit of home away from home here for Andy," Jane said, in a tone of voice that neither Andy nor Jane had heard before. She put Baby Nancy down on the floor, letting her toddle around the room a bit.

"Yeah," Andy chimed in, getting into the spirit of the lie, "they even got me this great mood tape — *Sounds of the City*." She pushed the PLAY button on her tape deck and the room was suddenly filled with the noise of trucks rumbling by and horns honking.

"Oh my," Andy's mother said, laughing. "It certainly is realistic. But what's this over here?" she asked, pointing to a grouping of half a dozen floor cushions (secretly borrowed from other rooms on the floor).

"Oh that," Jane said casually. "That's our little conversation nook. Andy told us how close your family is and how you try to get together as often as possible to sit down and talk things over. And well, we knew it would be a good idea for us, too. And so every night, we have a 'Sharing Hour,' where we open up with each other about the little stuff of our days — the joys and frustrations. It's one of the ways we have of staying close, and not getting too lost around here."

"Yeah," Toby said, forcing herself to contribute here, trying to see her shyness as a horse she was determined to get on and just ride. "When we first got here, Jane and I missed our own families like crazy. It was really Andy who showed us that we could make a little family right here. I don't know what we'd do without her."

"Well, isn't that sweet," Andy's mother said.

"Jujube!" Baby Nancy said, running full-tilt across the room and grabbing onto Jane's leg. Jane, secretly enjoying this attention, picked up the littlest Cord, and admitted, "It looks like I've got myself a new friend."

Charles, who had been standing at the window, surveying the campus below, wondered aloud, "Are there a lot of cute black girls around here?"

Ted's curiosity took another direction. Pointing toward the ceiling, he asked, "What's the deal with the teabag?"

No one knew quite how to answer that.

Mr. Cord's concerns centered on food.

"Do you think that Ye Olde Inn, which we're staying at, has a decent restaurant, or should we just try some of that delicious food you've been telling us about right here in the cafeteria?"

"Oh, sorry Dad, but we can't," Andy said quickly. "It's a shame, too, because they really put out a spread on Friday nights. Lobster tails, usually. But I'm afraid our housemother, Alison Cavanaugh, has invited us all up to her penthouse apartment for a dinner she's fixing tonight. It's the kind of thing she's always doing, throwing little parties for her girls."

There was not one single ounce of truth to this. Although Alison was a wonderful person and a devoted housemother, she had never been known to cook anything more adventurous than Lean Cuisine and tea in the tiny kitchenette of her apartment on the top floor of Baker. Even when she had romantic candlelight dinners with her boyfriend Michael Frank, Canby Hall's guidance counselor, it was Michael who did the cooking.

This dinner was strictly the brainchild of the three culprits from 407. They had done the shopping in Greenleaf the day before, and spent all morning putting the meal together. Alison had agreed to all this mostly because she was happy to see some spirit of togetherness among them. Plus, the roommates had promised to do her laundry for the next three weeks. Alison didn't usually drive such a hard bargain, but her pride demanded some repayment for having to pose as the cook in a 1940s-style flowered apron the roommates found for her at the Country Trends Thrift Shoppe in town. They felt the apron was the incredibly perfect "homey" touch.

The whole meal was designed around the idea of "homey," so that Andy's parents would get to thinking she really did have a home out here. They fixed roast chicken and corn muffins and cranberries, and an apple pie for

dessert. Andy was the chef. All the years helping in her family's restaurant gave her the
know-how, and Toby and Jane were willing
helpers. Although the dinner was a lot of work,
they wound up having fun together. Fixing a
whole meal in such a tiny kitchen was a
comedy of errors and the three of them really
got into the goofiness of the situation. And
because all this togetherness was just an act,
they could all let themselves go and enjoy it.
It didn't count, so no one's pride was at stake.
On Monday, everything would go back to the
way it was, but for now they could just enjoy
the situation.

They even found they shared a common
sense of humor. In the kitchen after dinner,
clearing up the dishes, their knees buckled
when they started laughing at the mere
thought of what would have happened if the
Cords actually *had* had dinner in the cafeteria that night.

"Can you just imagine my father coming
face to face with those steam tables?" Andy
said, tears rolling down her cheeks. "A great
chef like him, seeing that police line-up of
food suspects?"

"I know," Toby said. "I've had stuff off
chuckwagons that was a far sight better. That
whatever-you-call it down there — sometimes
it's hard to tell whether you can just eat it
right off the bat, or whether you better think
about killing it first."

"That's why there's always a knife lying around on the counter," Jane said. "In case one of the server girls has to stab something quick."

"Well, I think we did pretty well by comparison," Andy said. "Or rather Alison — that Julia Child of Canby Hall — did. And she's being so charming to my parents! I think they really think I'm in good hands. And the room — you guys really did a job on it. The Three Bears didn't have a cozier room." She stopped for a second, then said, "Uh oh."

"Uh oh what?" Jane asked, suspicious.

"Well, speaking of the Three Bears reminded me that Goldilocks wants to stay with us tonight."

"Huh?" Jane said, not getting it yet.

Andy explained, "Baby Nancy wuvs her Jujube. She wants to stay with her tonight."

"So you said yes," Jane guessed.

"Come on. You'll love it. She only has to be taken down to the john three or four times during the night."

On Saturday, the roommates split up, taking charge of the various Cords. Jane took Baby Nancy on a walk to the skating pond which, at this time of year, was filled with ducks. Baby Nancy loved feeding the ducks with torn-up hunks of stale bread that Jane had brought along with them. She also enjoyed collecting "treasures" she found along the way and deposited in her plastic pail. These included pine cones, bottle caps, and earthworms.

Toby had drawn responsibility for the two Cord brothers, and had arranged beforehand with Randy to take them horseback riding. When she asked if he had any mounts tame enough for a couple of city boys, he told her, "Well, we've got Daffodil and Daisy. Both so old we haven't seen them move in a few years. We think they might be dead. It's hard to tell."

"They sound perfect," Toby laughed.

And they were. Though the Cord brothers were city tough and streetwise, when it came to horses, Daisy and Daffodil were plenty thrilling enough. Toby and Randy followed them along the trails, kicking the pace up to a light gallop over the flat open fields, slowing the horses to a walk through the dense patches of forest. The long ride also gave Toby lazy, easy time to be with Randy, to talk with him about her loneliness here in Massachusetts. He really seemed to understand. And to care. And he didn't once mention the difference in their ages. Which Toby took as a very good sign, although a sign of what she wasn't quite sure.

Meanwhile, left to his own resources, Andy's father wandered over to the dining hall. When he saw what was being passed off as "lunch," he tracked down Mrs. Sharp and spent the rest of the afternoon helping in the kitchen, demonstrating for the cooks the latest techniques he had picked up at restaurant conventions, promising to send Mrs. Sharp copies of his pamphlets on "Magic With Macaroni" and "First Aid for Hamburger." By the time they parted, he and the head dietician were great friends, and the future of cuisine in the dining hall was a little brighter.

Andy spent most of the day alone with her mother, shopping out at the mall by the highway. Shopping was their way of being together. Back in Chicago, either at home or around the restaurant, there were always too many of the other family members around for them to have real, private talks with each other. If they wanted to have a deep discussion or talk about a problem, they went shopping. Often on these trips, they didn't buy anything. It was just a way of being alone without being too heavy about it — so whatever they wanted to say could just sort of come out naturally.

Which was just how it happened today. Somewhere between Andy getting a new pair of running shoes and her mother picking up a terrycloth bib for Baby Nancy that said HERE COMES TROUBLE, they stopped for a sundae at the ice cream shop.

When they'd both decided to pull out all the caloric stops and go for it with cherry-marshmallow sundaes, her mother asked point blank, "How much of this little show did you girls trump up for our benefit?"

Andy swallowed hard and admitted, "Most of it. Are you mad?"

Her mother shook her head. "No. If you really want to stay here so much that you'd go to all this trouble, and if all your friends were willing to go along to help you stay here, then only the show is fake. The spirit behind it must be real, or you couldn't have pulled it off. I don't like lies, but I think we pretty much forced you into this one. We just wanted so much for you to come back home, that we wouldn't accept that you might actually be happy here."

Andy thought for a moment before revealing the whole truth. "There *are* a few problems," she admitted. "Jane and Toby and I are not the easiest roommates. We've actually been pretty prickly pears with each other. I think we'll work it out eventually, but there's been some rough going."

Her mother smiled at this, and said, "You know, I'm actually a little glad to hear that. It would just be a little *too* unreal if everything were as perfect as this presentation you've been putting on for us. Like that science fiction movie where everyone's so nice it's unreal, and it turns out it's because they're not real people, just pods. Frankly, I'd rather hear you were having a few adjustment problems than that you were all a bunch of pods out here."

"You know," Andy said, "if there weren't this big table between us, and if we weren't in public, and if I weren't so concerned with being cool, I'd jump right over there and hug you for being the absolute greatest, most understanding mother between Chicago and Massachusetts!"

Sunday morning, when the Cord's station wagon pulled out through the gates of the campus heading for the highway, the three roommates dropped the hands they'd been waving and grinned at each other, flushed with their success.

"Well, it looks like we did it," Jane said. "They didn't tie you up and stuff you in the back of that Volvo and drag you back to the Windy City. Apparently we persuaded them you're really okay here, and that they'll just have to live without you until Christmas."

"It was touch and go for a minute yesterday, though," Andy joked. "I thought for sure my dad was going to move in and take over the cafeteria and turn it into the Canby Hall of Steak and Ribs!"

"You know, come to think of it," Toby mused, "I think that in the end we were in greater danger of *them* staying here than of *you* leaving. Baby Nancy had to be practically torn from her Jujube's arms. Ted discovered that the pond here is full of dozens of new varieties of frogs. And Charles added the phone numbers of six girls to his — is it okay to say 'Little Black Book'?"

Andy smiled. "Yes, Toby, it's fine. I hope we're all done with that sort of thing — being insulted when nobody meant to insult anybody. I mean, I think this weekend has shown us that we can afford to have differences and tease each other from time to time, don't you? I mean, so what if I think you're a little bit of a slob and a snob, Jane? And so what if Jane thinks you're from Hicksville, Toby? What's important is that now we're all friends, and real friendship can stand up to little differences. Right? Jane? Toby? Hey, where's everybody going? Hey, I'm sorry. Oh no, what have I done?"

As the other two walked away, Jane up to the room, Toby off toward the foothills, Andy stood alone feeling hopeless, like she had spent days perfectly wrapping a beautiful present and, with one stupid move, pulled it all apart like a slipknot.

CHAPTER SIXTEEN

Dear Charlotte,

Oh do I need sisterly advice — and fast!
When I called Saturday everything was going
fine with Andy's family. We really did a great
job for her, if I say so myself. And selflessly!
With all the running around getting ready
for her family, I completely forgot about my
quiz on irregular verbs in French. I think I
got two wrong. And you know how I hate
getting anything less than A's. But did she
appreciate this? No! As soon as her family
was gone and everything was okay, what did
she do but turn around and first insult me (I
won't tell you what she said), then insult
Toby on my behalf! Of course, this was all
in a joking around kind of way, but still. . . .

Or do you think I'm being too sensitive?
I'm sort of always on edge, about a particular
someone to be exact. I haven't told you about
him. I'm not sure why. Well, actually, I *am*

sure why. It's that I can't imagine you'd approve of him. And Mother and Father would be horrified.

I know what you're thinking — that he's something mildly unacceptable. Like that he's not interested in banking. But it's much worse than that! And worse in so many ways. For one thing, he's a rock musician. For another he wears an earring. Do I have to go on?

I could never bring him home. Or to dinner at the Hunt Club. There's no way to make him suitable. He deliberately tries to be unsuitable and scruffy and generally weird. It's his rebellion against his family — Boston bluebloods who go back practically to the Mayflower. I thought people stopped rebelling in the 60's.

I can hardly think of anything but him. I especially have difficulty thinking about Neal, which is another part of the problem. Can a girl have two boyfriends at the same time? Does she have to let them know about each other? Does Cary Slade (that's his name — isn't it a *wonderful* name?) even count as a boyfriend yet? Why do I like him so much?

Please call me as soon as you get this. I'd call you, but my phone credit card is already smoking, I've been using it so much, and I'm afraid Mother and Father are going to throw a fit. I need to know about Cary. And I need to know about Andrea and October and what to do about the dismal situation between us.

The thing is that I was actually getting kind of attached to them. Once I got down off my high horse, I started to see that it can be fun to have roommates — even if they're mega-different from me (well, not quite as different as Gigi Norton, please!) But now everything's gone wrong with us again, and I can't think of how to put it back to rights. And I'm not all that sure I want to. They probably feel the same way, and so we're all sitting in our separate corners — me burning and Andy probably feeling like an insensitive jerk and Toby feeling rejected. What a mess.

Well, let me know if you have brilliant solutions to either problem. Being in college, you ought to be further along in both these sorts of dilemmas — romantic and social.

Your loving sister,

                                        Jane

P.S. Do *you* think I'm a slob?

CHAPTER
SEVENTEEN

While Jane was sitting in the fourth floor broom closet (about the only spot in Baker where a girl could get any real privacy), scrawling her letter to her sister, Andy was in the dance studio running through a furious set of warm-up exercises, tears streaming down her flushed cheeks. Toby, meanwhile, was running all the way to the Crowell farm, to find a friend who wouldn't think she was a hick. When she got there, though, only his two younger brothers were in the yard.

"Randy around?" Toby asked, trying to sound casual, which was no mean feat, considering she was both upset and out of breath.

"Up in the hayloft," the taller of the gangly boys said, motioning up at the top of the barn.

"Maybe I'll pay him a visit," Toby said, trying to keep all emotion out of her tone. She could tell that these two were devilish and would give their brother an awful time of it if they thought she was a girl friend.

She went into the dark, woody-smelling barn and climbed the ladder. When she came up into the loft, Randy was there. He heard her and turned and stopped pitching bales up against the far wall. He just leaned against his pitchfork for a moment and studied her seriously. "Something's wrong," he said.

Toby nodded and, in spite of hating it when she cried, she began pouring tears. Randy set the pitchfork against the rough plank wall of the loft, came over, put an arm around her, and sat down with her on a stack of hay bales. He didn't say anything, just now and then brushed the tears from her face with the back of his hand. It was just the comfort she needed — strong and solid and silent. He was like her. He knew when words weren't necessary.

"You really are my friend, aren't you?" she said, when she had pulled herself back together a little.

"Yes," he said.

"I've never really had one like you. I guess I didn't think I could be close like this with anyone. Especially with a guy."

"Funny things happen all the time," he said, "usually when you're least expecting them. Like this. You came all the way East to a girls' school and found a cowboy for a friend."

Toby nodded, thinking about this.

"Now tell me what's got you all riled up," he said, giving her shoulder a friendly squeeze.

She told him the whole story and then waited while he thought it over.

"It sounds to me like your friend Andy just did the old Two-Step."

"What's that?"

"Oh you know — Open mouth wide. Stick in foot. She probably feels worse than you and Jane combined. My guess is that you three will get past this little snag. You're just all so oversensitive, it's going to take a while to build trust."

"How come you know all the answers?" she said.

He laughed. "Oh wow, believe me, I really don't! I've just been through a few more years than you."

"Oh no. Here we go again with the 'Mr. Older and Wiser' routine. Can't we just leave the subject alone for once, and just be regular friends, on equal footing?"

"Okay pardner," he said, mock-seriously shaking her hand. She had never felt so close to him as she did at this moment. These were strange and new feelings, and before she knew it, she said, "Randy. Would you like to do something with me tonight? Go to the show or something?"

When he didn't say anything right away in reply, she rushed in to fill the pause. "Oh, it wouldn't be like a date, or anything."

"Yes," he said, very slowly and carefully. "It would. Which is why I don't think we should do it. You just have to trust me on this, October. And you have to understand that it doesn't mean that I don't care about you. Because I do."

But Toby didn't hear any of the last of this. She was already down the ladder and halfway across the farmyard.

Later that day, Dee Adams came back up to her room, exhausted from skateboarding through the entire Sunday afternoon, covering practically every path on the Canby Hall campus.

"Message for you," Maggie said, looking up from her biology workbook, in which she was reluctantly reviewing the parts of the earthworm. "Toby left it for you earlier this afternoon. I stuck it in the corner of your mirror."

"What does it say?"

"I don't know. I didn't read it. Or rather, I *forced* myself not to read it. Not reading any of your mail or messages is one of the efforts I'm making so that I have a noble character."

Dee pulled the folded-over note out of the mirror frame and went over to her bed with it, teasing Maggie along the way by keeping it in its tight folds.

"You make fun of me," Maggie said, "but I'm not kidding. If there ever is a Greatest

Roommate in the World contest, I fully expect you to enter me."

But Dee was already flopped onto her bed, puzzling over the note.

"Now what do you suppose this means?" she asked Maggie, then read aloud: " 'How would you like to come with me and see the BEST ocean — tonight!' "

"Well, didn't you tell me something about the two of you going to the shore next weekend? Wasn't she trying to cure your homesick blues?"

Dee hopped off her bed nervously and grabbed her hairbrush off the top of the dresser. She stood in the middle of the room vigorously running it through her long straight blond hair — first front to back, then bending over and brushing it down from the nape of her neck to where the ends almost touched the floor.

Maggie sat silent and waited. She knew this was what Dee did when she was deep in thought. Usually, it brought her to some conclusions, but this time, when she put the brush down and shook her hair back over her shoulders, she just shrugged at Maggie.

"We talked about going out to the ocean here, but I told her it would only be a pale substitute for me — that what I needed was the real thing, my old Laguna Beach stomping grounds. So I don't think by best, she means the Atlantic. But she can't mean the Pacific, either. I mean, we do have the little three-thousand-mile-gap problem. No, it's a mystery message for sure. I'll have to go next door and ask her for a decoding."

But when Dee poked her head into 407, only Jane was there, sorting her sweaters into neat stacks on the floor in front of her dresser.

She looked up and asked Dee, "Do you think I should arrange them by color? That's what I've done with my socks here." She opened the top two drawers to show Dee how they were filled with neat little folded-over pairs.

"Jane Barrett!" Dee said in fake shock, pressing her hand to Jane's forehead, as if testing for fever. "What's come over you? Don't you think you ought to go over to the counseling center? I mean all this sudden neatness could be the warning sign of a total nervous breakdown. It's just the sort of thing that happens in the movies, just before the teenage daughter finally cracks. She starts being real weirdly tidy."

"That's what I love about this place," Jane said, "all the support a person gets for mending her ways. All that's happening is I'm through being a slob. From now on I'm going to be a model of neatness. If some Army drill sergeant wanders in, she won't find *one* thing to criticize. I'm even going to learn to make hospital corners on my bed."

Dee said, "I'm pretty sure that if you just take two aspirins and go to bed, you'll be

better in the morning. By the way, have you
seen Toby?"

Jane shook her head. "Not since this afternoon. Cary and I were taking a walk and
ran into her coming through the Maple
Grove. It wasn't really much of a meeting.
She's barely speaking to me now that Andy
told her I think she's an unsophisticated hay-
seed. You know, I had the feeling that something was bothering her — something more
than just the trouble between us. She seemed,
well — distracted."

Dee was, at this moment, a little distracted
herself. She was looking beyond Jane, up at
the ceiling above Toby's bed. Something —
or rather the lack of something — had drawn
her eye up there. A sixth sense maybe. And
so she wasn't really surprised when she saw
what she knew would be true — Toby's teabag was gone.

Dee didn't say anything about this. She was
pretty sure Jane hadn't noticed, and didn't
want to call her attention to it. She wasn't
sure how much she wanted to say to Jane just
yet. If Toby was up to something — and it
looked like she was — Dee knew she'd be
sending another message. She'd just have to
wait and see what it was.

CHAPTER EIGHTEEN

By eight that night, both Andy and Jane were sitting in silence in 407. Or rather, they were sitting in two very different kinds of silence. Andy's was a nervous quiet that came from not knowing what to say that wouldn't make an already bad situation worse. Jane's was a protective cover for wounded pride. Not only was she still stinging from Andy's insult, but in the two hours they'd been back here together, Andy had yet to mention how nice the room looked in the wake of Jane's major clean-up campaign.

Andy, for her part, *had* noticed and *was* appreciative of Jane's attempts to change. She was just afraid that if she congratulated Jane, it might be taken as sarcasm. By now, she was at the point where she worried that if she said "hi" to Jane, it might get taken the wrong way. She didn't even dare put on a tape, not even really low. She was so afraid of aggravating Jane again that she was even trying to turn the pages of her American lit book softly.

Both of them were also, in their silence, mulling over another problem. Toby. Where was she? They hadn't seen her since this afternoon, and she had not exactly been in a calm, happy frame of mind then. Each of them was half waiting to hear her footsteps outside the door.

But the next footsteps to stop outside the door of 407 were fast ones, flapping in shower sandals. They belonged to Dee, who rushed breathlessly into the room, then stood holding onto the door frame and said, "Toby just called me. She's in Greenleaf. She's planning to head West on the Night Flyer. I guess it stops at the depot in about an hour."

Before either of the roommates had a chance to respond, the phone rang.

Andy picked up and, after a brief pause, handed the receiver to Jane. "Cary Slade."

"Hi," he said to Jane from the other end of the line, shouting over a background commotion of clattering dishes and clanking pots and pans. "I know this probably isn't any of my business, but I thought you'd want to know that your cowgirl roommate is here at the diner. She's sitting at the counter with a cup of coffee and a train ticket in front of her. Seems to have rather immediate travel plans."

"Yes, we just found out. She called a friend and told her she's heading West."

"She wanted me to come along," Dee interjected. "Said she'd go to Laguna Beach with me first, then head back to Texas and find work on a ranch somewhere. She doesn't think she can go back to her father, that he'd be too angry. The thing is, she doesn't even have enough for train fare. She's got a ticket to Denver. From there she's planning to 'ride the rails.' I mean, it's a totally insane scheme."

Jane asked Cary to hold, then looked questioningly at Andy.

"What do you think we ought to do?" she asked her.

"Maybe we shouldn't interfere," Andy said.

Jane nodded and said, "If she really wants to go back West, maybe it's for the best. Maybe the three of us would *never* get along, anyway."

"She probably knows something about riding the rails," Andy added, trying to reassure herself. "It's probably not as dangerous as it sounds."

"Are you kidding?" Dee said. "If it's what I think it is — it's hitching a ride on a train. That's not only dangerous . . . it's, it's. . . ."

"Even if we did go after her," Jane said, trying to sound sensible, "we'd probably just all get in trouble. Sunday night curfew is nine-thirty and it's nearly nine now. And what would all the trouble be for? A girl who probably hates us and would be just as happy to never see our faces again."

"You're probably right," Andy said, trying to sound as if that settled the issue.

"Are you guys completely crazy?" Dee shouted suddenly. "Are you going to let pride about your dumb differences keep you from seeing what's really happening? Toby's leaving because she's miserable and alone and feels shut out by you two. And you can bet she doesn't know a *thing* about riding the rails. That's something out of Western novels and movies, not real life. Get a grip, will you? She's out there calling for help and you're turning up the Walkmans in your heads!"

Andy and Jane looked at each other, and it was as if an electric current passed through the air between them. Suddenly all their differences melted away and in this moment they saw with one set of eyes. They both saw that what Dee was saying was true, that Toby needed them, and that they needed her. If she *did* get on that train tonight, the friendship they'd nearly come to have would disappear forever, along with the train whistle, fading away into the night. Jane was the first to ackowledge out loud the huge wave of understanding that was passing between them.

"Dee's right," she said.

"I know," Andy agreed. "So," she added with a smile, "what are we waiting for?"

Jane put the receiver back to her ear, afraid Cary might have hung up by now. But he was still there.

"Do you think you can stall her until we get over there?" she asked him.

"I don't know. What do you want me to do — get out my guitar and play her 'Don't Fence Me In'?"

"Oh, you'll think of something. You're the smooth talker. You kept *me* from getting away. See if you can do the same with her."

"Well, I'm not going to have the same motivation, but I'll try my best," he promised, and hung up.

"I'll come with you guys," Dee offered when Jane was off the phone. "I never mind risking a little trouble. And I really care about Toby."

Jane thought for a moment, then said, "If you wouldn't mind, I'd like this to be just Andy and me. I want Toby to know her roommates really want her back. And besides, that way you and Maggie can help us get back into the dorm. If you could wait down in the first floor linen room for us, I'll bring along a flashlight and signal for you to open the window from the inside."

"Wow!" Dee teased. "James Bond stuff!"

"I think I might have got it from a story about a girl detective," Jane admitted, pulling on her running shoes.

When she and Andy were off, down the back stairs of Baker, Dee rushed to the outgoing phone downstairs, pleaded her way past the three girls lined up for it, and made a fast call to the only Crowell she could find in the book. She knew enough about Toby's interest in Randy to think that getting him to come to the train depot might add a little extra persuasion on top of Andy and Jane's.

"You know," Jane said to Andy as they jogged along the side of the road into Greenleaf, "I've never done anything like this before."

"Anything like what?"

"Well, like breaking curfew. I don't think I've ever broken a rule before. I don't think I ever even disobeyed my parents at home."

Andy's eyes opened wide with amazement. "Girl, you've *got* to be kidding. Never did anything wrong in your whole life? Come *on*. You must have. At least once. Think hard. You've got to be able to come up with at least *one* little crime."

Jane thought hard for a long moment, then a grin began to spread slowly across her face.

"Aha!" Andy said. "I knew it! What was it?"

"I can't tell," Jane said. "It's too embarrassing."

"You've got to. Part of the new policy here is open communication. This is your rite of passage into the inner circle of our friendship. You've got to tell me."

"It's pretty terrible," Jane said.

"I've got a feeling I can handle it," Andy said.

"Well," Jane started hesitantly, "when my sister Charlotte was eight and I was four, she got a Barbie doll for Christmas — with about eight outfits and the little beach set and all. I got a baby doll. I was insane with jealousy. And so I waited until everyone was asleep on Christmas night and then I went downstairs and took Barbie from under the tree. And I gave her a crew cut."

Andy exploded with laughter. "I love it," she said.

"Okay now," Jane said, "your turn. Fair's fair."

But they were almost to the diner by now, and so Andy promised to tell her story later.

"As soon as we have a slow moment, I'll tell you all about the day I sat up in the tree for a whole day and nobody could talk me down out of there. I could be a real brat when I wanted. Uh oh. Looks like the diner's closed. The sign's off and there's only one dim light inside. Toby can't still be there."

"No, but Cary might be, and he'll probably know where she's gone to."

The two of them pressed their noses to the window of the diner and peered in. There in the back, Cary was wet-mopping the old linoleum floor.

Andy turned to Jane and said, "The work day in a restaurant's never done. Believe me, I know. But I thought you said this guy's ultrarich. What's he doing here?"

"Oh. Well, he thinks the diner is real life,

and he wants to be a part of it. He feels like his parents cushion themselves away from real experience with their money, and he doesn't want that to happen to him."

Andy nodded.

"You don't think that sounds dumb?" Jane asked.

"No."

"I guess I don't, either. But it's the first time I've thought about it. Cary's making me think about a lot of things in new ways. I don't always agree with him, but never knowing what he's going to say is an interesting experience. With my old boyfriend — I mean my boyfriend back in Boston — I always knew we'd agree on everything. This is just real different. I'm still not sure what to make of it. Or how Cary Slade's going to figure in my future."

"But you don't have to," Andy said, draping an arm around Jane's shoulder. "That's one of the great things about life. You don't have to live it all today."

Jane smiled and said, "What you mean is what we've got to worry about *now* is Toby."

"You've got it, girl."

Jane knocked hard on the window until Cary looked up. He put the mop back in the roller bucket, came and opened up the door.

"You just missed her," he told them. "I tried to stall her as long as I could. Told her all my longest jokes. But she said she had to catch a train, and split about five minutes ago. If you want to get her, run. The Flyer's due in any time now."

Andy and Jane ran as fast as they could for the depot. Then felt a little foolish as they barreled in to find no train in sight and Toby sitting calmly on the old wooden bench. She seemed astonished to see them there, and to not make any connection between their presence on the scene and hers.

"You guys are out kind of late, aren't you?" she said.

"Toby, we've come for you," Jane said.

"But why?"

"We want you to come back with us."

"I don't understand. You don't even like me."

"That's not true," Andy said. "When I said that about Jane thinking you're a hick, I was only trying to lighten things up a little. I'll admit I did a pretty rotten job. But all I was really trying to say was that we're different from each other, but not different *bad*. And not too different to be friends. When Jane and I found out what you were planning to do tonight, it really shook us up. I don't think it hit us until then how far we'd come toward really being friends."

"You mean like the Crystal Gayle song about how you never miss a good thing till it's gone?" Toby said shyly.

"Right," Jane said. "Look, I know I'm the one who got everything off to a terrible start. I just couldn't get over not having the room to myself. And then by the time I did, it was too late. Too much had been said. But then over this weekend with Andy's family, I started to see how much fun it could be *really* being roommates. Now I'm ready to be a real roommate — if you two will have me."

"My," said Toby, sparing as ever with words.

Andy knew a joke was risky here, but it was hard to tell what Toby was thinking, and the beam of the Night Flyer was now visible coming down the track. At this point, she figured anything was worth a try.

"Toby, please," she said. "If you won't stay for your sake, do it for me. If you leave, I'm going to have to get along with Jane all by myself."

Amazingly, it worked. Jane laughed and Toby grinned and nodded.

"Okay," she said. "I guess if you took the trouble to come fetch me, it'd be mighty rude to send you packing. Kind of like being stuck in an avalanche and saying 'no thanks' to the St. Bernard. So if you're both willing to give it another try. . . ."

"Not just *another* try," Andy said. "A *real* try. If problems come up, we don't all run off in different directions, we stay and talk them out. Agreed?"

"Agreed."

"Agreed."

And they put their hands on top of each other's to symbolize the new start. And then they watched as the train pulled in and let on an elderly woman and a man with a small boy, then pulled out again, heading West. Without October Houston aboard.

As the sound of the train receded into the distance, the sputter of Randy Crowell's ancient pick-up truck grew louder coming into the parking lot behind them.

"I heard someone was leaving on the Night Flyer," he said out the window of the cab. "Must've been wrong."

Toby walked over to him and said, "I got my mind changed for me."

"Good thing," he said, "because I would've missed you a lot."

She looked at him skeptically.

"It's true, October. I consider you my true friend."

"But nothing more," she said.

"Look. I'm twenty. You're fifteen. I think that's a fine age difference for friend-friend, not so great for boyfriend-girlfriend. So why don't we try being friends for a few years. And then if you get to be twenty and I'm twenty-five and you still think I'm so irresistible or whatever, maybe we can have a talk about it."

She had to smile at this speech. "Irresistible?" She made fun of him.

"Well, I *am* pretty cute," he said. "From certain angles. My right ear is definitely cute."

"Hey!" someone called, running toward the

depot. It was Cary. "What happened?" he said, winded from the run.

"Well, we talked her into giving us one more chance," Jane said. "Now we've got to get back to Baker without getting all three of us in trouble."

"I know," Randy said, "hop in back. Burrow under the hay. All of you. No one'll see you there."

And so they rode all the way back to campus like that. And under the cover of all the hay, Jane and Cary shared their first kiss. It was the best kiss she had ever experienced. And so she tried one on him. And it was just as good. She knew these kisses meant she'd have to think about this relationship with Cary. And rethink her relationship with Neal. But as Andy said, that could wait until tomorrow.

When they got to the gates of Canby Hall, Randy cut to his parking lights and glided the truck up the drive as quietly as he could. When he got to Baker, he helped the others out of the back. Jane signaled with her flashlight and the window slid open.

"Whew! They're there!"

The three roommates made a run for it. It was easy getting through the window, which wasn't too high. But as soon as they were in the linen room, they heard footsteps. Probably Alison making night rounds. All five of them — Andy and Jane and Toby, plus

Maggie and Dee, quickly covered themselves with sheets from the shelves and flattened themselves on the floor.

This was not, of course, good enough to fool Alison.

"Could I see who my ghosts are?" she said, throwing on the overhead light. The five let their sheets drop. Alison stood there for a long moment before saying, "Please don't tell me the whole story. Just tell me this. Does this mean that I'm not going to have any trouble from 407 for the rest of the year?"

Toby and Andy and Jane all nodded their heads vigorously.

"And I am not going to hear about any more surfing parties in the fourth floor washroom?"

Dee and Maggie shook their heads just as vigorously.

"Then I think I'm just going to go to bed and forget I saw you all. I suggest you do the same."

Later still, in 407, with the three roommates in their beds with the lights off, Andy said, "You know, maybe it's some kind of weird tradition with 407. Maggie told me that her sister and the other two girls in here before us had a hard time at first, then became really good friends."

"Well, if that's the tradition," Jane said sleepily, "then we'll probably become the three greatest friends Canby Hall has ever seen. Because we sure have had the hardest time getting started. I'll say one thing for tonight, though, it has given me an even better new experience to write about for my class assignment. In fact, it might be the first time in history a Barrett has ridden in the back of a hay truck."

"You know, there's just one more thing on my mind," Andy said. "I was wondering, Toby — now that we're all being open with each other — if you'd let us know what the tea bag meant."

But Toby's only response was the deep breathing of a soundly sleeping girl — a Canby Hall girl at last.

JUNIOR HIGH

Coming soon from Scholastic — just in time for the back-to-school season — a brand-new series, JUNIOR HIGH!

Meet the latest crop of Cedar Groves Junior High eighth-graders on their very first day of school. Join them in the chaotic cafeteria, the crowded corridors, the craziness of new classes. Get to know the students — from inseparable best friends Nora Ryan and Jennifer Mann, to the impossible class nerd, Jason Anthony; from rich and beautiful Denise Hendrix, to sports maniac Mitch Pauley and sarcastic Susan Hillard. Share experiences with these eighth-graders — the triumphs and setbacks, the friendships and first loves, the adjustments, the fun, and the occasional pain. Most of all, become a part of Cedar Groves Junor High, and the nonstop action that happens there.

You won't want to miss JUNIOR HIGH!, so watch for these titles:

Junior High Jitters (October 1986)

Class Crush (January 1987)

The Day the Eighth Grade Ran the School (March 1987)

Read All About
The Girls of Canby Hall!

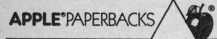